The Dream Weaver

I0602293

Antonio Williams

Cadmus Publishing
www.cadmuspublishing.com

Published by Cadmus Publishing
www.cadmuspublishing.com
Port Angeles, WA

ISBN: 978-1-63751-308-8

TABLE OF CONTENTS

CHAPTER 1

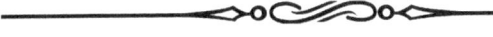

I don't give a damn what you told them you were gonna do," he yelled at Mom. "I need the money to get back what I lost." Standing not much taller than mom, 'Big Thomas' looked down at her unforgivingly.

"Thomas you can't do this to him again," mom pleaded, "I promised him this would be his month to get some new things; and we need to fix that raggedy bunk bed they're sleeping on." Mom, a short petite woman with rich, even skin, the color of coffee beans, with large eyes and a round face that lit up when she smiled; reminded me of the sun being blocked by rain clouds at times like this.

"You shouldn't have made that promise without checking with me first; and there's nothing wrong with that bed. There are kids in this neighborhood sleeping on the damn floor every night!"

I knew right away that the broken promises had to do with me. I've been coming home from school with an old Scholastic book catalog for months now and one day I showed mom some books I really wanted. For me, reading was just like watching Mr. Roger's Neighborhood, my favorite show, only better. I really wanted those books and the new shoes she was going to get me. But I was used to wanting, so I could wait another month. Besides, I hated how mom looked like a powerless child when Thomas yelled at her.

"Now go get the money before he gets here; I want to meet him outside," Thomas ordered. Mom quietly stepped across the peeling linoleum kitchen floor to the old decrepit carpet in the living room my siblings and I were now sprawled on, and went to their room down the hall. Neither my little sister, Lisa, my older brother Tommy nor I looked up as we watched an old episode of Mr. Roger's Neighborhood on a TV that only had eleven working stations, enjoying the increasingly rare evenings the three of us were together. We weren't the kind of family that acted like bad things never happened in our home; we'd seen more than our share. No, it wasn't that, we just knew when to mind our own business. So, like usual, we acted like we heard nothing and saw nothing but Mr. Roger, even though we heard and saw it all.

Mom always told us to never get involved in her and Thomas's fights, even if they were physical. She always said, "If I couldn't handle it I wouldn't be with him." For some reason we accepted that, so none of us ever got involved... except Lisa. She was the only one of us who wouldn't − couldn't stand by and do nothing when things got physical. If she was around she had to "stand up for momma," as she put it, until Tommy or I pulled her away and explained to her the way mom explained it to us.

I wanted to go to mom and tell her it was okay, I'll wait till next month just so she wouldn't have to argue with Thomas anymore But I knew that would just make things worse. Mom came back to the kitchen with a wadded up bundle of money and reluctantly put it in Thomas's waiting hand. Then she went back to their room without another word. Thomas left the house, the screen door slamming behind him like it always did.

Tommy started in on me as soon as Thomas was gone. "You shoulda never told mom about those stupid books, Tony, you know how hard it is on them right now dad's been trying to get a car so we don't have to walk to school and back every day. I know you like walking with Katy but I want a ride." My brother was two years older than me, but those years only seemed to aid his physical development; they did nothing for his mind. He wasn't the sharpest but he was lovable. Not at this moment, though. I looked at him with enough steam to blister skin.

"Her name is Kadence and I haven't talked about those books in over a month! I know how hard it is. I don't think you do, though; Thomas is always giving you new stuff. Why don't you tell him not to get you anything else until we have a car?!" He smacked his lips and laughed derisively.

"Stop playin', you know dad gets that stuff for free from those zombies." He had me on that one. Thomas never gave anyone any money for the things he brought home for Lisa and Tommy. Luckily Lisa came to my rescue, saving me from sounding petty.

"Books aren't stupid; plus I like when Tony reads at night – it's lke being at the movies," she said. "I wish he could get some new ones; we've read all the Dr. Seuss books. What about the Bernstein Bears again, can you read one of those tonight?"

Reading aloud while we lay in our beds at night became a ritual for us when I was about seven. My teachers told mom it was uncanny how quick I picked up new words. Since we all share a room Lisa won't let me skip a night when she's home and not at grandma's house.

"Actually, I was thinking we could start on this new book I checked out from the school library called Frog and Toad." The argument with Tommy was quickly dropped when I responded to Lisa. She always had that effect on me and everyone else.

"Yeah, that sounds funny," she said with three quick claps of her tiny hands and her beautiful smile that spread across her whole face. People often thought we were twins but since she didn't have my thumb-sucking problem and the resulting overbite, I didn't think so—she was much prettier. Mom came out of her room and told us to get ready for bed and we all got up and proceeded with another one of our nightly rituals: smothering mom with hugs, kisses, and "love you"s until we were all on the floor laughing and giggling.

After we brushed our teeth and washed our faces we retreated to our room. I read two chapters before Lisa fell asleep. I thought Tommy was sleep too, until his voice drifted up from the bottom bunk. "You really got into that story tonight huh? You actually got me into it —that was good."

"Lisa really likes it when I read with feeling —it's called inflection. She says it helps her picture the story in her mind like a movie. Glad you liked it too." I smiled in the dark.

We were both quiet for a minute until he spoke again, sounding more like an innocent kid than ever. "I didn't mean what I said about your book earlier… I know you haven't gotten any new stuff in a while. I just hate seeing Mom and Dad fight that's all… I know it's not your fault, though." He sighed.

"I know Tommy. We'll be alright," I said in my ever-optimistic voice.

"When Tony? When will we be alright, 'cause it seems like it's never gonna change. I'm sick of Spaghetti O's and baked beans and you've had those raggedy shoes way too long. Man, I'm tired of living like this!" We had this conversation more and more lately. Although he's older, my precociousness made me feel like the oldest in times like this. Just like I helped him and Lisa with their school work when they needed it, I knew what to say in these moments.

"We just have to be patient. Once we get old enough we can get our own jobs and then we can take care of Lisa and ourselves. And once the snow starts falling we can go out and start shoveling like we do every winter and make some money to help out Mom." I said it with so much conviction because I really believed it—I had to. "Besides," I continued, "we don't have it that bad. Look at JJ across the street—he's been wearing the same clothes since we've known him." I once caught JJ taking a bird bath in the school sink. When I saw him he just shrugged and said he usually made it to school before everyone else. I never said anything to anyone and he started talking to me when he saw that I didn't shame him.

"We just have to be thankful for what we have," I finished, reciting what Mom always told us.

"Yeah, you're right. We better get some sleep… Goodnight, Tony." I blinked away my tears and rolled on my side, not saying goodnight back because I didn't want him to know that I was crying.

I awoke to the sound of the screen door slamming shut and for a moment I thought I was still dreaming because I usually slept through the door slamming and all the other sounds that drifted through our thin walls. Then I remembered that the screen door didn't slam in my dream house. I heard Thomas' voice and knew for sure I was awake. Man… I turned over to my left side facing the door with my eyes open, listening as if looking at the closed door would make my hearing better.

"Felicia?" Just by the way he called my mom's name I knew there was going to be trouble. "Felicia, what happened to the other hundred? I thought you get three hundred a month."

"I do Thomas," she replied as if she'd been expecting this at precisely this time.

"Well, what happened this month?"

"They made a mistake with the checks, Thomas; even Teresa didn't get her whole check."

"What? That sounds like some nonsense to me. You must think I'm stupid. Where's the money?"

"I told you Thom—" The familiar sound of Thomas's hand making contact with Mom's face rang through the house, cutting Mom's words short. Then the noise of dresser drawers being thrown open and the tiny closet being ransacked followed.

"Please, Thomas, don't do this tonight," my mom pleaded, "we can call the check place on Monday and get it straightened out."

By this time I knew Lisa and Tommy were wide awake too. "Come here Felicia." There was a brief silence. I held my breath, anticipating another slap. Instead the sound of fabric ripping, silence and then Thomas's humorless chuckle. "So you changed it up on me; you hide it down there now, huh. Do you have any idea what kind of situation you put me in tonight?"

"Thomas, your son needs some new shoes. Don't you care that he's walking around with shoes that have holes in them?"

A smack louder than the first one was the answer. Mom yelled, and from the sounds Thomas was making, started fighting back. Their door slammed open and Lisa jumped out of her bed, opened the door and started yelling in her high voice. "Momma, stop hitting my momma!" They were in the hallway and with our door now open, I could clearly see Mom on the floor crying.

"Lisa go back to bed baby, Momma's alright." Tommy was up too, walking towards Lisa, ready to bring her back to our room. Mom looked up from where she was on the floor, with iron defiance and said "Please, Thomas, don't do this in front of the kids." She said it with just the right emotion—not anger but condemnation—so that he heard something else, something that tipped him over the edge.

Lisa was clinging to mom at this point. I was sitting cross-legged on the top bunk and Tommy was a few steps from the hall. Something about those words set Thomas off; his face went dark with humiliation and I knew he was about to hit mom again and I didn't think he'd stop this time. I could see Lisa trying to bury her face into Mom's partially nude upper body to escape the blow. I have to get involved this time!

I scrambled to the ladder of the bunk bed, moving so quickly I forgot that there were only two rungs in the middle and they were very weak. As I stepped on the first rung, one side of it gave in, I released my grip thinking to jump the rest of the way down, like I usually do, but the top rung had clamped onto my foot and snagged me. My ankle twisted and instead of falling to the floor I swung down top first and smacked my forehead on the railing of the bottom bunk. Please don't let Thomas hit my little sister, was my last thought before everything went dark.

As I gradually opened my eyes, I was met with a surreal sight: I found myself seated upon the softest, most velvety carpet I had ever touched. Its pristine cleanliness was mesmerizing, as if it had been meticulously cared for by an unseen hand. Directly in front of me, an empty wooden rocking chair swayed gently, as though someone had just risen from its embrace. The room itself was suffused with a radiant glow, making every object within it seem almost otherworldly.

As my eyes adjusted, I couldn't help but marvel at the brilliant brightness that enveloped the space. The room was imbued with an uncanny iridescence, akin to stepping into an ethereal realm illuminated by the purest white light. It was as though every element in this small space was pulsating with life and vibrancy. Upon closer inspection, I noticed a fascinating peculiarity: the entire room appeared to be intricately crafted from delicate threads of string or yarn, woven together like an elaborate tapestry. The effect was both mesmerizing and unsettling. Each thread seemed to hum with a subtle energy, creating a mesmerizing dance of movement throughout the room. Even the walls bore the appearance of a tightly woven quilt, each stitch seemingly alive, producing a remarkable and bewildering sensation of a living, breathing entity.

The room emanated an oddly familiar aura, as if it held a secret connection to my past, a nostalgic feeling that tugged at the edges of my consciousness. My gaze fell back to the living carpet beneath my feet. Its gentle undulations made it feel almost sentient, as if it were an organism unto itself. The whole environment seemed to breathe and pulse with an enigmatic force, leaving me in awe and wonder at the inexplicable spectacle before me.

A door that I hadn't been aware of—or had it just appeared?—opened and in walked the most beautiful woman I have ever seen. She had the skin of smooth dark chocolate, her lips were full and slightly pink and her eyes were shaped like almonds with long eyelashes. Her hair was long—at least to the middle of her back and very curly with an unnatural shine that made it look wet. She was wearing an all-white gown that covered her figure. I noticed she had a small bundle of black yarn and a golden crochet needle in her hands as she walked in front of me, then sat down in the rocking chair and began humming and knitting. I almost thought she didn't know I was there until she spoke.

"Do you understand int, Tony?" she asked without looking up from her weaving. Her voice was so sweet-sounding, yet clear and firm. But her lips weren't moving; she was still humming at the same time. The effect was so delightful I couldn't help but smile as I replied. "I... I don't know," I almost whispered and then found my full voice that seemed so crude in the presence of this lovely being. "The only thing I can think of is... this must be a dream. I mean how can the carpet and even the walls be moving!" I finished in an amazed yet bewildered tone, while softly rubbing my hands across the carpet. I was more fascinated than afraid of it.

"A dream is nothing more than a misunderstood reality; a glimpse of the past, the future, and the eternal present; a symbol that holds the key to many doors of knowledge," she said.

"So I am in a dream?" I asked as my courage grew.

"Yes. But so is everyone else."

"Does that mean none of this is real?" I asked, somewhat dismayed at the thought of never seeing this lovely woman again. She looked up and smiled.

"My child, this is the only thing that is real. The world is one big dream, weaved from the purest substance there is. You must open your mind to see between the strands of physical embroidery—your dreams are real and they have the power to manifest." She looked back down at her knitting and I tried to digest what she just told me, then she began communicating in that same beautifully serene voice again.

"In the world you know they say all matter vibrates; that is true everywhere. What you see in the carpet and the walls here,

Tony, are vibrations—the underlying power that animates all life, including you." I suddenly got the urge to look at myself in a mirror. I glanced down at my hand, still softly rubbing the carpet and for a split second I couldn't distinguish my hand from the floor! It looked like I was being absorbed into the carpet. I snatched my gaze away and focused back on her.

"Who are you? What's your name?" I blurted out.

"I am Neith." It sounded like weave except with an n instead of a w.

"Neith, are you God?" I asked hesitantly.

"Some call me by that name."

"Does that mean I'm dead then, since I'm talking to God?" I asked the question in such a depressing and defeated tone that it made her smile as she continued to weave.

"No child, nothing is dead. And you… are more alive than you have ever been—now that you know."

"I hope I don't forget you, Neith," I said sincerely.

"Many have because they have forgotten their true selves—." She looked into my eyes intensely, "But you won't Tony. You won't."

"Where are Lisa and my mom?"

"On their way back," she replied with the same maternal joy I often heard in Mom's voice.

"Back, they were here too?" I asked. "Are they okay?" The memory and panic of the night resurfaced.

"Yes. Everyone has been here before and they will return."

I looked around, still mystified, and then it hit me: this is my room, just much more vibrant. I was so busy trying to make sense of it all that I didn't notice she had stopped knitting. Without a word she got up from the chair and kneeled in front of me on both knees. She motioned for me to do the same, so I got to my knees too. She stuck the needle into the ball of yarn and held it out to me.

"Take it; it is time for you to weave your own dream."

I reached my hand out to grab it, but as soon as I touched it, it seemed to draw itself into my palm and vanish. I looked back up into Neith's face and she was a lot closer than before—our bodies were nearly touching. I felt a powerful energy radiating from her as she bent down and kissed me on my forehead then embraced me the way a loving mother—like my mother—would embrace her child.

"There will be times when you will feel more alone than anyone else. When you do, look within yourself and you will find me: I am always with you. You are never alone."

Tears started running down my face as I began to cry softly. Soon my tears were flowing so steadily that they clouded my vision; the more I blinked the blurrier things got. Finally everything went dark and all that remained was the residual feeling of comfort, safety, and the power of Neith's embrace.

I slowly opened my eyes and winced at the sharp brightness of my surroundings. My eyes slowly acclimated to the light and I was able to keep them open without wincing. I shifted my eyes around, taking stock of the room that I quickly recognized as a hospital. I tried to sit up but stopped immediately—my head felt like what I imagine bowling pins feel like after being run over by a bowling ball. Then I heard Mom's voice coming from the side of the bed.

"He's awake, Lisa, go find the doctor. Tony? Hey baby how do you feel?"

I tried to respond but all that came out was a croak that vaguely sounded like "alright." She stepped out of view and I heard water running, then she came back with a cup in her hand. She pushed a button on the side of the bed and my head began to rise. She stopped it at an angle I would be able to comfortably drink from without choking, and then held the cup to my lips. I took a sip then reached my hand up and held the cup myself and gulped the rest. Mom was watching me with motherly concern the whole time.

"Take your time, Tony."

"'I'm alright Mom. Where's Lisa?"

Just then Lisa came in followed by a tall, dark, bald guy with glasses and the longest beard I've ever seen. He had on a maroon sweater, a stethoscope around his neck and a clipboard in his hands—he looked nothing like the doctors on TV, I thought. A very pretty Asian lady came in with him and checked the fluids in my IV and read the technical numbers and signs on the monitors.

"How do you feel, big guy?" he asked in a thick African accent.

"I'm ok... my head aches though."

"I'm sure it does; you had a nasty fall. Well, I'm Dr. Kampala and I'm going to ask you some questions and run through some simple tests to make sure everything is still working right. Are you up to it?"

"Yeah," I said.

He went through a list of questions like what's my name, when my birthday is and what school I go to. And then he asked me what the things he just asked me were. I repeated the questions a little shame-faced thinking he must've thought I wasn't paying attention because I was staring at his beard. He had me touch my finger to my nose, follow his finger with my eyes; then he held the stethoscope to my chest and back and had me breathe deeply. Finally he checked my head which was heavily bandaged. When he finished he made a sound of approval.

"So do you remember what happened to you, Tony?"

"Yeah, I was trying to get out of my bunk bed too fast and my foot got caught and I fell; the next thing I remember is waking up here."

And Neith, but I didn't tell him that—he might think I was crazy. I also didn't say why I was in such a hurry to get down. I knew telling him that Thomas was about to hit my sister while beating my mom would only make things worse.

"Well, you hit your head pretty hard big guy—" Dr. Kampala began. "You've been out for three days. We thought you may have had some swelling in your brain so we ran some tests but didn't find anything other than a small fracture. You seem to be healing quite well and there doesn't seem to be any permanent damage done. Now you might develop migraines or other symptoms so we'll be keeping a close eye on you for a little while."

"I've been sleep for three whole days!" I said in true astonishment, not really concerned about the other stuff he said because besides the now-slight pain in my head (the nurse put something in my IV that made everything seem slight) I felt fine.

Dr. Kampala got up and started talking to Mom on the other side of the room as Lisa's sweet little voice sang out.

"I hope your head doesn't stay this big; it was already huuge."

I looked down at her giggling face and couldn't help but laugh with her. "You haven't seen me in three days and this is how you treat me," I said, pretending to be hurt.

"I got you something," she said after she stopped giggling.

"Oh yeah, what'd you get me?"

"Close your eyes," she demanded as she ran over to the chair her and Mom had their coats on. "Keep them closed," she said.

"They're closed," I said patiently.

"Okay, you can open them now." She had a copy of the book Frog and Toad Together, the sequel to the book I started reading to her the night I fell.

"What! You got this for me?"

"Well, more like for us since you'll be reading it to me at night." She said it so matter-of-factly I smiled.

"Thank you, lil sis—" I said around a yawn. "How did you get it?"

"Well you know Momma gives me a dollar when I help out around the house… I've been saving them up. It didn't even cost that much." She finished, sounding quite proud of herself for finding a good deal. "Are you going to sleep again? How could you want to sleep again—you've been sleep for three days."

"It's the medicine they gave me," I said in a drowsy voice.

"Well, sweet dreams; I love you," she said as she stood up on the bottom part of the bed and kissed me on the cheek. "I'ma pray that your head gets small again…"

❖   ❖   ❖

I awoke later that night. The nurse helped me up to use the bathroom and they brought me some food. I found a channel on the TV that was playing Mr. Roger's Neighborhood; it was a new episode too. Before I got into it I heard a knock at the door and Thomas's voice call out my name. "Tony, are you up?"

"You should really let him rest, Mr. McNeil," the night nurse said.

"I won't be long, I just want to say goodnight to him."

"Alright," she capitulated. "Let me see if he's awake first." I thought about playing sleep, but decided not to.

"I'm up," I said as the nurse came into view.

"Alright, your dad is here to see you, but I told him to make it quick because you really need to rest, the plump nurse said maternally.

"Okay," I said as she left and Thomas walked up to the bed. When I looked up at him I immediately saw how old and tired he looked. He had a timid look on his face as he started talking, like he thought his voice might make me worse.

"Hey son, are you alright?"

"Yeah, Thomas, I'm fine," I said in a low voice, then looked down.

"Listen son, I'm so sorry for what happened —" The pain in his voice made me look back up at him. "I know this is all my fault and I wish I could take it all back but… I know I can't. I know you guys probably think I don't love your mom but I do — I love her with all my heart. Things are just really hard on me right now. But things are going to change, though, I'm going to change; I promise that." He pulled me over to him and hugged him. "Do you believe me son?"

"Yeah, I believe you." And the truth was I did believe him; I had a strange feeling that things were going to change and so was he.

"I'm going to go, but I'll be back in the morning with everybody else." He bent down to the floor and came back up with a pair of brand new Nikes. "These are yours. I'll set 'em over by your clothes. I love you son."

"I love you too Dad." I lay awake for a while, thinking about how things used to be when I was younger —when things were happier. We didn't have much back then either, but we spent more time with each other, Mom and Dad never fought and we were really happy. I went to sleep with happy thoughts on my mind... and Neith.

The next day around noon everybody was in my hospital room and we were all talking and getting along. Even Mom and Thomas seemed to be getting along okay — we were like a real family again. As soon as Tommy came in he hugged me, looked me up and down and said, "You're gonna be alright lil bro; you're as strong as me... well at least your head is anyway." We both laughed, but I knew he was worried and this was confirmed when he suddenly grew serious and said "I was scared for a minute, Tony. I didn't want you to die or turn into one of those kids stuck in a wheelchair. I'm glad you're okay." I didn't know what to say to that so I showed him my new shoes.

"Those are the new AirMaxes," he said with sincere admiration as he rotated them in his hands. "Yeah, Dad gave them to me last night." He smiled at me calling Dad "Dad" instead of Thomas. I used to call him Dad when I was younger, but when I was about eight I saw him hit Mom for the first time and just started calling him by his name. I guess I just saw him as a different person. He didn't even seem to notice or care.

A firm an authoritative knock sounded out and whoever it was didn't wait for an answer. In walked a serious-looking European lady with greying blond hair pulled back in a severe bun; round rimmed glasses with some kind of decorative chain connected to them hung from her neck. She wore a thick wool skirt that reached down to her shoes and a brown jacket over a white top. She looked like a mean principal at a mean school. When she was sure she had everyone's attention she began to speak.

"Hi, my name is Carol Johnson, I'm with the Child Protection Agency and I would just like to ask, um… Tony, Thomas and Felicia some quick questions if that is alright." She looked up from her notes ,and then looked at everyone in the room with a forced smile. Mom walked over to Carol, extended her hand and said, "I'm Felicia, this is Thomas and Tony of course," she finished, waving at Dad and me. "Tommy, take your sister outside for a little while please." Without a word Tommy took Lisa by the hand and led her out.

We were all familiar with child protection or "Them People" as we called the police and every other government agency. We always heard stories of other kids being taken from their families by child protection and never seen again (no one ever told us it was probably a good thing for most of them). We would come home one day with an overly dramatic story of how one of the neighborhood kids had gotten taken by "Them People." Thomas would say, "See, that's why you gotta keep them people out of your business; ain't no tellin' where they took that boy. He'll probably never see his family again."

Mom even sat us down one day after her and Thomas had a nasty fight, and lectured us on keeping our business to ourselves. "We're a family," she began, "We might have issues from time to time but all families do. The important thing is that we take care of each other and don't put anyone else in family business. If anyone ever comes to the house trying to ask questions about us, all you ever need to tell them is we love each other and there aren't any problems." So in our minds the Child Protection Agency was the enemy.

"Well, you might not know this but," Carol Johnson began as she sat down, "anytime a minor is seriously injured in the home and hospitalized it is mandatory that the hospital notify us, so that is why I'm here." She paused to let us absorb that bit of info. "My job is to make sure the child is in a safe environ—

"He is. All of my kids are, in fact." Thomas cut in. She looked at me, tacitly asking the obvious question: how did this happen then? She didn't have to speak it though, Thomas understood the implication clearly—we all did. Mom, noticing the mounting tension, interceded.

"Listen, Miss Johnson, we understand why you're here, so you can ask all your questions and we will answer them to the best of our ability."

"Thank you," she replied, "I'll make this quick." Turning to me she asked, "Do your parents hit you, Tony?"

"No."

"Do you feel safe at home?"

"Yeah, my family won't let anybody hurt me."

"Was your injury caused by something other than an accident?"

"No. I fell off my bunk bed." She asked all three questions with not a hint of emotion and I gave my answers in the same manner.

"Miss Rawlins, Mr. McNeil, were you home when Tony's accident occurred?"

"Yes. His father and I were in our room when we heard the commotion; we immediately investigated and called the ambulance." Mom answered for both of them in her professional tone.

"Alright, thank you for your time and I hope you get well soon Tony," she said as she got up.

"No problem," Thomas said as he watched Carol Johnson leave my hospital room. "Damn, they could've at least sent a black woman or a white woman with some personality. If I was scared, she would be the last person I'd talk to!" Thomas finished his rant as Lisa and Tommy came back in. With the child protection lady gone, the tension dissipated and we all relaxed.

CHAPTER 2

A week later I was back at home and things seemed to be better than before: Thomas was home more often and he hadn't yelled at Mom once; he even took us all shopping for new clothes which truly surprised us all. My eleventh birthday came up and Mom cooked a big meal: cornbread, macaroni and cheese, baked chicken, and an Oreo ice cream cake... all my favorites—no Spaghetti O's or hot dogs. Physically I was doing well, my wound healed and the doctors told mom I could be more active again. There wasn't a night that went by that I didn't dream of Neith; I remembered more and more of my first encounter with her and I looked up every word she used that I didn't know. I understood more every day and I think I began to have an idea of what she was telling me.

I was thinking about it as I walked home from school with my friend. "I've changed my mind—" she announced, "I'm going to be a therapist for kids when I get older. My mom says kids are the future of the world, so we have to make sure they're raised right so they can be good at running the world." Kadence wasn't considered pretty and though she had her own group of friends, she wasn't one of the popular kids either; but she was all of that to me—she was my best friend. We always talked about how life would be when we grew up; what we were going to do and where we would be. We helped each other with school work and we both got good grades. She is a year older than me and mature for her age but it's her kind heart that stands out the most.

"I think you mean a mentor, like Mr. Evans," I said.

"Yeah, I think that is what it's called," she said with an appreciative smile.

"I want to help people too," I said, "but I don't know what job I want yet; I have to do some more research." We crossed the street and made it to Kadence's block. This is usually where we part ways because her dad doesn't allow her to be alone with boys. So we stand on the corner for a few minutes, talking before she goes inside and I continue my walk. This is also where the last couple of nice blocks were, with nicely painted houses, clean streets and nobody hanging on the corners except parents meeting their kids as they got off their school buses. It reminded me of the real life Mr. Roger's Neighborhood. When I crossed over to my side of town, even the trees looked different; with thinner trunks and premature leaf loss as if they felt the same poverty the people living there suffered from.

"I think you would make a good mentor," I told her, "You're really good at helping people and people like talking to you."

"Well, I think you should be a teacher—you're really good with words," she said.

"Yeah, but nobody really likes teachers," I complained, looking down at my shoes. "Maybe I'll be a librarian, so I can be around books all day."

"That's not true, people love good teachers. Besides, you shouldn't worry about whether people like you as long as you're doing the right thing; that's what my mom says. And librarians are always old and wrinkled." I looked up at her and smiled, but quickly dropped it as I noticed the look on her face.

"Man, here comes my dad!" she said in a voice filled with terror, but eyes narrowed in defiance. I turned around and her big muscle-head dad was almost on top of us. I thought about running but I couldn't get my legs to move. "What'd I tell you about being alone with boys?"

"Tony isn't like that, dad." Kadence protested.

"Oh, I get it: you think you're grown now." His voice was calm and steady as he continued. "As long as you live here, in my house, you will do as I say. Do you understand?"

"Yes." Kadence spit out through her clenched jaws.

"Oh, you're mad huh? No you're not, but I'm a give you something to be mad about. Now get in the house, lil girl." Kadence stormed off but looked back at me with wide eyes.

"And you…" he took a menacing step forward and continued in the same calm tone; the aggression was solely in his rigid stance and unblinking eye contact. "I know what's on you lil boy's minds. She's not the one...stay away from her." He lumbered off and quickly caught up with Kadence and silently scolded her as they disappeared in their house. I stood on the corner for another minute or so, still scared—more for Kadence than me. What did her dad think was on my mind? I started walking home and my fear was soon replaced by a steel determination to make sure Kadence was safe.

That night I went to sleep in a hurry. I don't know how I did it, but the thoughts that were in my head as I nodded off played out in my dream. I thought of Kadence and her father, and then different scenarios that were linked together by clear thread began flashing through my mind like so many scenes in a movie. I reached out with my mind and grabbed the ones that I thought would make Kadence the happiest. I drew from the emotion she gave off when her father showed up on the corner. I imagined her dad struggling to hold up a huge metal weight and then slowly being pinned down by it. His threatening posture and unblinking eyes that remind me so much of Thomas when he raised his hands towards my mom, was crushed out of him as the weight lay on him. The strands of fear and dread were cut out, leaving her dad stranded in the furthest reaches of her mind as if he were a suppressed memory. I replaced her fear with feelings I knew her to have when sitting at the lunch table at school with her girls: The day I saw her do an impression of one of the teachers and every girl at her table laughed so loud the other kids at the next table looked their way. Her eyes sparkled with carefree happiness and her confidence was infectious. I focused on those feelings, enhancing them by showing her her own strength and beauty; knitting together a future she believed in implicitly. When I was done I watched it all play out. The sparkle in her eyes shined brighter and a protective barrier of strength radiated from her, repelling doubt and fear as she went through her days striving towards her goals. She looked up and I felt her eyes lock on to mine so I waved, but she didn't wave back. I released her dream then retreated back into myself, sleeping through the night peacefully.

Consciousness returned, and with it every muscle in my body tightened, my jaw clenched, making my teeth grind and my fingers curled into an unbreakable fist. I heard someone yelling and then I blacked out. I woke up on the bottom bunk feeling really stiff, like I did that day at school after I got a cramp in my leg in gym class—except this was a cramp in my whole body. Mom was holding my head and Tommy was pressing my body down as I lay on my side. His eyes were wide as he stared at me.

"What are you doing to me?" I groaned.

"You just had a seizure, Tony. Are you hurt anywhere?" I heard Mom say through the gaps of her fingers that were over my ears.

"I'm stiff… my muscles feel like I just had one big Charlie horse in them, but I'm fine."

"The doctors said you could develop some after effects; I was really praying you wouldn't," Mom said worriedly. I did remember them saying something about migraines, but what was this!

"You guys can let me go, Mom." They both released their hold on me, but Mom told me to stay lying down for a while as she walked out the room. I rolled on to my back and looked at my brother.

"What happened?" I asked.

"I felt the bed shaking and at first I thought you were playing around because you were making this funny grunting sound too. But when I looked down at you and saw how you looked… I knew something was wrong, so I jumped off the bed and called Mom. She ran in and told me to hold you down on your side and she held your head still. You looked like one of those possessed people in a scary movie," he finished and stopped pacing while giving me a long stare from the corner of his wide eyes. His usual bravado and teenage invincibility that had his round shoulders naturally straight was gone. Now his athletic posture combined with his wide eyes made him look like he had just been startled by someone hiding behind a corner. "You don't remember any of it?"

"Not really. I heard a yell, but that's it," I said, as I wiped some sweat from my forehead.

"Man, I'm glad we switched bunks. You would've split your head again if you were still on top."

Mom came back with a cup of water and some pills.

"Tommy go grab a wet washcloth please—cold water," Mom yelled as he darted out the room. "Here, take this: it should help with the stiffness and help you sleep." Tommy came back and handed Mom the towel that was a little too wet, and she wiped the sweat from my face, neck, and chest.

"Listen," she began, "you go back to sleep and tomorrow morning we'll go see Dr. Kampala."

"Alright," I said.

"Keep an eye on your brother, Tommy," Mom said before she kissed me and Tommy then left.

Tommy told her he had me and then he jumped back up to his bunk with some of his old swagger. When we were both settled back in our beds I asked him if I was really that scary looking. He said that I definitely was and he was glad Lisa wasn't here because she would've had nightmares. Seeing how he was genuinely shaken up, I was glad she was at Grandma's; I definitely wouldn't have wanted to scare her. I yawned loudly and said goodnight.

"Man, I'm not going to sleep; you might start shaking again!" he said.

"I'm fine Tommy, but you can stay up if you want to. Goodnight." With that, I rolled over and was knocked out soon after.

The next morning Mom's friend, Bernadette, took us to the doctor's office. They ran a bunch of tests, put some wires on my head and laid me under a loud machine. "Well," Dr. Kampala said, "there is definitely increased activity in your frontal lobes; that is consistent with the pattern of a grand mal seizure."

"What does that mean Doctor?" Mom asked. "What caused it?"

"Seizures occur when neurons—brain cells—rapidly fire at random and out of sync with the rest of normal brain activity. As far as there being a trigger… We haven't figured that out yet, but grand mal seizures are indicative of epilepsy and that could be a result of the trauma from his fall. This could turn out to be a one-time delayed reaction or it could end up being something like temporal lobe epilepsy, in which case these seizures could become frequent." Mom absorbed the information with a straight face, arms crossed as though she were trying to hold herself together. I was still enchanted by the way his long beard moved whenever he spoke.

"We'll just have to keep a closer eye on him." Dr. Kampala patted my knee and smiled. The wrinkles at the corners of his eyes held an intelligence that said he knew the effect his beard had on kids. "For now, though, I'm going to get his test results examined by one of our neurologists."

"Thank you Doctor," Mom said as she shook his hand.

"My pleasure Miss Rawlins, and you take care, big guy."

By the time we made it home school was out. Tommy was in the living room eating some chips, watching the new TV Thomas recently bought.

"You're not gonna die are you?" he said around a mouthful of chips.

"No, Tommy, I'm an epileptic."

He asked me what that meant so I explained it to him the way the doctor explained it to me, but emphasizing that the seizure could've been a one-time thing.

"Man, I hope you don't have anymore… you know you farted when I was holding you down and it was bad!" We both busted out laughing until my stomach hurt and Tommy was almost choking on his chips. "Hey, your friend Katy was looking for you today," he said after he recovered.

"Kadence. What did she say?" I asked a little guardedly, thinking he was going to make a mean joke.

"She just wanted to know where you were. She seemed kind of worried about something." He looked at me and gave me an awkward wink. I sighed with as much exasperation as I could muster and he went on. "I told her you had a doctor's appointment and you'd be back tomorrow."

I thought about our walk home yesterday and my annoyance was replaced with worry. I don't know if Kadence's dad ever hit her, but he most definitely seems worse than Thomas—a lot bigger too. I didn't let Tommy see my concern, though.

"Yeah, I'll see her tomorrow," I said with a small shrug of my shoulders.

That night, Thomas ordered a couple of pizzas and we all ate in the living room. "Alright, y'all, I got a surprise," Thomas announced after he gulped from a can of beer.

"I thought this was the surprise—we ain't had pizza in years," Tommy muttered next to me.

"We're getting a new car in a day or two," Thomas went on, apparently not hearing Tommy's comment.

"Finally, thank God!" Tommy shouted in my face, with his hands clasped as if in prayer, then he turned to Thomas, bright-eyed and asked, "What kind of car is it"

"A black Benz of course," he replied with a straight face. We all looked at him until he chuckled. "Nah, just kidding. It's a grey Jeep Grand Cherokee, clean and in good condition. It was a deal I couldn't pass up."

"Well, that will definitely help out a lot around here," Mom said and kissed him, "A Benz wouldn't fit all your kids in it."

That night I think we all went to sleep feeling good, but I couldn't help thinking about Kadence. I was anxious to get to school.

The next day I didn't see Kadence until lunch; she was sitting with her usual group of girlfriends. When she saw me she got up and came over to my table.

"How—"

"Are you—?"

We both spoke at the same time. I let her go first.

"How did your appointment go?"

"Fine, they said I might be epileptic, so I might have seizures sometimes," I gave a slight shrug as I said it.

"Really? Does it hurt when you have one?" she asked with concern.

"Nah, but I only had one and I didn't even remember much of it. My muscles just felt stiff, but it wasn't that bad." I paused for a second, "So… Tommy told me you were looking for me yesterday; he said you looked bothered. I'm sorry I got you in trouble."

"It's not your fault; my dad is just psycho. He grounded me for two weeks and made me do a lot of chores. That's not what I wanted to tell you though," she paused, then brought her voice to just above a whisper and leaned across the table a little. "I had a crazy dream last night, but… it wasn't just a dream."

My heart was pounding so hard I could hear it. Could my dream really have reached her?

"What was the dream about?" I asked in the same whisper, trying to keep the excitement out of my voice.

"I don't want to talk about it here. Walk me home after school and I'll tell you on the way home."

"But what about your dad, won't he—?"

"We won't have to worry about him today," she cut me off and looked away as she said it, "just be there after school." She got up and went back to her table.

I didn't know what to think, but I couldn't help being distracted for the rest of the day. When the school day was finally over I hurried up to the side of the school where Kadence and I usually met. We both almost bumped into each other.

"You ready?" I asked her.

"Yup."

"So, tell me about the dream," I said as we started walking. It seemed she was just as eager to tell someone because she didn't seem to notice my impatience.

"I was so mad at my dad when I went to bed that night. I mean, I do really good at school—you do too—so I don't get why he wouldn't want us to be friends," she paused with a long sigh, "anyway, when I finally fell asleep something weird happened," she paused again as we crossed the street. "I started having a dream like I've never had before, and I've had some crazy ones. But this one was like…like it was really happening or was going to happen. Does that even make sense?" She didn't wait for me to respond. *"I was older and I was getting ready to get on a plane to go to college. My mom was so proud of me as we hugged each other at the airport. She told me not to forget to take pictures for her. She was crying but I knew they were tears of joy because I could feel her happiness as she kept asking me if I remembered my toothbrush and the spare set of house keys. With each question she hugged me and stepped back like she could tell the answer from the way I looked. My dad was looking at me with the biggest smile I'd ever seen him have, but he didn't say anything to me and when I went to hug him he backed up. I laughed because I thought he was playing but when I tried to hug him again he took another step back. So I stopped and asked my mom why he kept backing away from me, why won't he hug me. And she just said who? When she said it he turned his back and walked away and disappeared in a crowd of people. I looked back at my mom and she just smiled and hugged me again and when she did I forgot all about my dad and I was happy without him.* All the bad feelings I felt when I laid down were gone; every thought I ever had about growing up and being successful got bigger and bigger until that's all I thought about. I was really happy."

"Man, that sounds like a really good dream," I said without meeting her gaze as we slowed our pace.

"I was really, really mad at my dad before I fell asleep, and it was like the dream... saw it and made him disappear. I forgot all about him, like I had never even had a dad. It felt so real. My dad is mean sometimes and a little crazy, but I still love him and I have a lot of good memories with him." She sighed. "He's not that bad really."

My heart dropped to the bottom of my stomach and I felt queasy.

"I didn't feel happy when I woke up from my dream; I felt like I had lost my dad and a part of myself," she continued, "I got up and went to the bathroom, and on the way to my room I heard my mom yelling, what's wrong over and over, so I ran in their room. My mom was on the phone with 911 telling them my dad was convulsing. I looked at him lying on the bed and," she wiped the tears from her face, "he looked like he was dying: he was shaking and one side of his face was dropping; like it was melting. I didn't know what to do."

"Is... he alright?" I asked as I wiped sweat from under my arms with trembling hands.

"My mom said he had a stroke; it's something like a heart attack, I think. They wouldn't let me see him after they brought him to the emergency room. My mom told me he's going to be okay, but I heard the doctor tell her he could end up disabled in some way." We made it to her corner and stopped. "I don't want my dad to die, Tony, or forget who I am."

I looked her directly in the eyes and told her that her dad wouldn't die and he would always remember her. The absolute sureness in my voice made her tilt her head slightly as she looked pack into my eyes. Then she told me there was something else that happened in the dream. She told me I was there.

"I couldn't see you but... I felt you looking at me. I can't explain it; all I know is I got a really strong feeling that you were there—watching everything." She inhaled deeply and let it out slow. "I don't know... I have to go now; we're going to see my dad. I won't be in school tomorrow."

As she turned to go I called her name and she stopped and turned back. I walked up to her and gave her a hug, she hugged me back and before we broke the embrace I told her again that her dad wouldn't die. She looked back at me as she walked off; her eyes glistening and a little red from her tears.

When I got home that evening I ate dinner in all but complete silence, answering questions succinctly and with little energy. I retreated to my room early, doing my homework and work I missed the days I was absent. Afterwards I sat in my bed in the dark, thinking of the dream I gave Kadence. How did I mess up so bad? I didn't really think my dream would come true, but it did and I missed up and missed something major.

I knew she was afraid of her dad at the time but... she wasn't afraid of him all the time. And that was it. I only drew from the feelings she felt at that moment: scared and mad at her dad for embarrassing her in front of me. I didn't think about how she felt overall, in fact, I really didn't think at all about how she really feels. That has to be it. Or maybe it wasn't me at all and I just witnessed it.

"Tony?" Tommy turned on the light, snapping me out of me reverie. "What are you doing sitting in the dark?" He was looking at me like he thought I might be having another seizure—tensed up and ready to spring into action.

"Nothing, I was just getting ready for bed. I'm fine; stop looking at me like that."

"You were praying huh? I pray sometimes too; it's okay. I just came to get some clothes. I'm staying at Deandre's for the night; I'll be back tomorrow night though." He went to the closet and took out some shoes.

"So I get the room to myself for one night—good. Lisa is coming back tomorrow too."

"Did you see your friend today?"

"Yeah, her dad had to go to the hospital last night; he had a stroke and he's still there." I couldn't keep all of the emotion out of my voice, so it came out a little bitter sounding. He said that's why I was so quiet tonight and praying just now, like he'd just solved a mystery. I told him yeah in a quiet voice.

"You really like her huh?" Before I could half-heartedly protest, he said I like everyone, though, and then he told me he'd see me at dinner tomorrow. And then he was gone.

Was it my dream that did this to my best friend's dad? Maybe I just dreamt what was already happening. That makes more sense—a premonition. But, what if… Well, there's one way to find out. Before I knew it, I was lying down with my eyes closed and I was soon sound asleep. I reached out with my thoughts and activated the dream world. I saw Kadence dreaming, but this time I didn't interact right away. Instead I observed and paid close attention to her emotions and thoughts. I focused my mind on penetrating the underlying feelings and thoughts she had about her life, so I could have a dream with a tighter connection to her overall emotions—not just what she experienced that day. When I felt I had enough input I began selecting strands from the different scenes that flashed across my mind.

I took a piece from one showing her dad giving her a gift and hugging her close; I attached a bit of another one of her dad and mom showing them as they were much older, holding a newborn baby while Kdance looked at them tenderly and they told her the baby looked just like her; and I grabbed a scene of her at some type of shelter sitting next to another girl, holding her hand as she talked. I carefully wove the strands into a tightly knit fabric, relying more on what Kadence's mind had revealed in her dream than on what I thought I knew. When I was done I watched it unfold and, again, she looked my way as if she could see me, but very quickly this time—the dream was so potent, so vivid and compelling that she was caught up in its reality. I released her dream and fell back into my own consciousness.

I felt pain in my muscles and tasted blood in my mouth. I couldn't talk or move, but this time I was conscious long enough to understand what was happening. I blacked out soon after my realization.

I opened my eyes and moved my head; my muscles were so stiff I had to force myself with every inch. Finally I made it to a sitting position on the bed and stretched out the rest of the stiffness. I reached up to wipe the blood from my mouth. Realizing that Mom and Thomas would be up soon I crept to the bathroom. I rinsed my mouth out and searched for the teeth marks on my lips or cheeks… there was nothing there. I didn't bite my tongue off like Mom said I could. So where did the blood come from? I rinsed my hands and the stinging sensation answered that riddle. I bit my thumb while I was sleeping. I dried off, found a Band-Aid and went back to my room. The last thing I want is Mom worrying and rushing me to the doctor's again. Besides, I think I knew what was happening: my dreaming was causing the seizures, and something was telling me to keep it to myself. So that's what I did.

"Boy, you look like you didn't get any sleep last night," Mom said after examining my face as we sat at the kitchen table eating breakfast together—a very rare moment.

"I did. I just stayed up late, catching up on school work I missed, but I'm not that tired." I was exhausted, but I wasn't going to admit it. Mom narrowed her eyes at me with a mixture of concern and suspicion.

"Did you have another seizure?"

"No, Mom—"

"Don't lie to me Tony."

I hated lying, but I knew I couldn't let anyone know about this.

"I just don't want you to hurt yourself again," she softened her tone, "and if there's anything Dr. Kampala can do, he has to know everything we can tell him. Okay?"

"I know Mom. I'm fine, though; I didn't have one." And maybe I don't want the seizures to stop—not if they're connected to my dreaming. I got up and put my empty bowl in the sink. Mom stood up too and hugged me like only she could: nestling me against her small body, making me feel protected—I almost fell asleep in her arms.

"Tony, I know you don't want me worrying but I'm your mother and that's what we do. I love you baby." I told her I loved her too and she kissed the top of my head and released me. I got ready then left for school.

Kadence wasn't at school today, but I was still ready for the day to be over with. I was so tired. After nodding off in two classes and sleeping through lunch, I was on my way home. When I arrived I was surprised to see Mom still home by herself. Lisa and Tommy still hadn't come home yet. I said hi to my mom.

"Boy, you look like you're about to fall out. Go and lay down till dinner." I assured her that those were my exact plans and then I asked her when Tommy and Lisa would be back through a yawn. She told me they'd be back for dinner and that Thomas was picking them up in the Jeep. She told me not to worry though; I had plenty of time to get a decent nap in. I told her I'd see her later then, sluggishly retreated to my room, kicked off my shoes and fell into bed.

When I woke up it was dark outside and the house was quiet... too quiet. It was way past dinner time and no one was here yet; even mom was gone. Well, maybe I could enjoy the quiet while it lasts. I found the casserole mom made and fixed myself a plate.

I was sitting in front of the TV when Bernadette and Mom came through the door. Bernadette had one arm around Mom's shoulder and was guiding her to the couch; Mom had her head down and was crying. When she looked up I stopped eating and rushed over to her.

"What's wrong? Why are you crying like that?" Her face was so puffy it looked like Thomas hit her over and over. She told me they were gone between sobs.

"Who's gone Mom? What are you talking about?" Bernadette was looking at me with her lips pursed and her eyes dim with sadness. "What happened Mom!?" I yelled. She focused on me as if she was seeing me for the first time and then snatched me up in a tight hug.

"Thomas had a car accident... Lisa and Tommy were with him. Thomas is in a coma. Lisa and Tommy didn't make it." She was crying and rocking me back and forth. My ears started ringing and I felt like I couldn't breathe. I forced myself out of my mom's embrace and ran out of the house; trying in vain to out run the words that just came from my mom's mouth. She couldn't have said Lisa and Tommy are dead! Everything was starting to get better for us; we were okay again. This can't be right. As these thoughts ran through my mind, the tears ran down my face. I walked and walked, head down and shivering from the cold, but not even caring.

"Tony!" I looked up and saw Bernadette in the street with her car door open. "Tony, come get in; you're going to get sick out here like that. Come on now, baby," she pleaded. I numbly walked over and got in the front seat of her car.

"I brought your mom to my house. You guys are going to stay with me for the night—you don't need to be alone right now." She turned on the car heater and we drove in silence for awhile.

"Tony, I know this is going to be a very hard time for you but you have to stay strong. Your mother is going to need you, now more than ever." She paused, turning a corner then she went on, "Sometimes things like this happen to people and they become more than they ever could've, had they not gone through it. You're going to make it through this and you're going to be stronger than you ever thought possible. In times like these we find ourselves more alive than we have ever been."

Something about that last statement penetrated the fog; it sounded like something Neith said. I looked over at Bernadette. She glanced at me and smiled warmly. When we pulled up to her house she led me in and made up the couch with sheets and a blanket for me to sleep on. She told me my mom was in the back sleeping and that I should do the same thing and she'd see me in the morning.

I lay on the couch and thought about Lisa and Tommy. I thought about Lisa's high pitched voice and the cute way she walked on her tippy toes and I thought about how grandma always favored her. I thought about how funny Tommy was and how much he enjoyed my reading at night and I thought about how Thomas treated him more like a son than me. I couldn't help missing them, loving them and resenting them at the same time. After tossing and turning most of the night, I got up and checked on Mom. She looked like a little girl... like Lisa bundle up with big fluffy covers, with nothing but her head showing. I swallowed my tears and focused on being strong for her—she needs me. I brushed her hair from her face and she grabbed my hand, and then opened her eyes.

"Tony... I'm sorry I can't be strong for you right now baby."

"You don't have to be sorry Mom; I'll be strong for both of us." I said it with a confidence I wasn't really feeling.

"You've always been the strong one, Tony. That's a gift and you're special because of it. I've known you were special since the day I had you." I asked her when Thomas was coming home. "I don't know if he is. They told me he might never come out of his coma, and if he does he probably won't have any control over his body."

I really didn't know how to feel about that; I was warring with trying not to blame him for everything wrong in our lives. But I felt guilty because the police told Mom it was a hit and run and Thomas wasn't at fault.

"Why wasn't he more careful with my babies in the car?" She hurled the question as if she sensed my internal conflict. "He took my babies from me… I hate him." She reached for me as she cried and shook from the pain. I hugged her back until she calmed down some. When she finally let me go she lay back down and softly cried herself to sleep.

Five days later we buried Lisa and Tommy; it was a small funeral: a few neighborhood and school friends. Mom seemed disconnected from it all; she was retreating within herself more and more every day. Kadence showed up with her dad. When we were outside of the church she spoke to her dad, then walked over to me and gave me a hug.

"I still can't believe it, Tony. I'm sorry."

"Yeah, it doesn't seem to be real. It's like a bad dream I can't wake up from."

"Are you okay?" she asked timidly.

"Yeah, I'm fine. Mom isn't doing so well, though. I see your dad is better—that's good." I tried to sound happy, but it came out high pitched.

"I wanted to talk to you about that too, Tony. I had another dream, like the one before, except this was even stronger, more real. My dad got better the same night and the doctors couldn't explain it. It was like nothing was ever wrong with him. They called it a miracle." She stopped and looked over at her dad. "You were there again, Tony... I felt it. It was just like we are now, talking. I could feel you there; I just couldn't see you. You saved my dad, didn't you?" She said it like she already knew the answer.

"How could I do that Kade?" I tried to make it sound like a 'yeah right.' I don't think it worked, though.

"I don't know, but you know something. You're just not telling me and I know it."

"Tell me how I could save your dad, but I couldn't even help my sister and brother?" I said it with the stomach-sickening bitterness I truly felt. I tried dreaming Lisa and Tommy back but they didn't have dreams anymore. I couldn't do anything.

"I'm sorry Tony—"

"It's not your fault," I cut in before she could finish.

"Are you coming back to school?" she asked.

"I'll probably take a couple of days off just for my mom, but yeah, I'll be back."

She hugged me again and looked me in the eyes. "Thank you Tony... I'll see you at school." Her dad came over and put his hand on my shoulder and lightly squeezed it, and then they left.

CHAPTER 3

"I could lose my job telling you this," she began.

He started to interject but she raised a delicate, finely structured hand to stop him and continued. "Let me finish. I feel like there's something strong between us; more than physical attraction. The way you look into my eyes it's… it's… so passionate, so real. I didn't plan on seeing you as anything different from the other guys in here but you are, and I can't help but notice it." She paused for a brief moment, looking down at the waxed floor. When she looked back up he met her beautiful brown eyes with an intensity that seemed to draw her closer to him.

Keeping his voice just above a whisper he responded. "The look I give you is me trying to let you see my heart and the way I carry myself around here is just me being true to myself. Thank you for taking the time to see the real me."

He looked around the well-lit closet, and then settled his eyes back on the blue work uniforms he was restacking on a shelf in the back. "So what do we do now?" He asked her as he knelt down to put the 6XL pants on the bottom shelf. "Before you even say it," he jumped back in, "let me assure you that I would never ask you to do anything to jeopardize your job or your freedom. If you lose this job I won't be able to see you for God-knows-how-long and I couldn't—wouldn't—put you through anything like this. But do we just let these feelings go? Give up what some people search a lifetime for just because your job title says it's wrong to act on these natural feelings we have for each other?" He shook his head and sighed then stood up and admired her toned body, lingering on her soft, full lips.

"That's why I'm telling you this now, Jason, I think we could—" she suddenly burped, then giggled hysterically as a German shepherd came in and started humping his leg. Then his mom appeared, he started crying and then... he woke up. Frustrated, again, it seemed that Jason could never finish the dream before it unraveled. He felt that if he could have the dream until it completed itself, it just might come true. He lay on his thin mat that constituted his bed and took stock of his situation. Jason Madison is 28 years old and he's been incarcerated since two months after his twentieth birthday for bringing drugs from Chicago to Minnesota and getting pulled over with them. He has a month remaining before he's released. He's done his time and he's ready to get out, although he doesn't have too much to look forward to.

From the age of six to fifteen he was in one foster home after another; group homes, shelters, juvenile treatment facilities— really any place that would take him. He wasn't a bad kid, he just had some issues. Both of his parents lost their parental rights or more like gave them up; his mom used drugs when she had him and his dad was addicted to the streets. He never felt like he fit in anywhere he went so he made it hard for people to like him let alone love him; that is until he joined a crew when he was a teenager. He started selling drugs, trying to make a living for himself' everything was working out—until he got caught. Once he was convicted none of his crew stayed in touch, the women that were so fond of his attention disappeared and he was on his own again; just the way it's been most of his life.

But Jason wasn't like a lot of the guys who came to prison and blamed everyone else for their problems; he took responsibility and accepted the fact that he was here because of what he did. His philosophy concerning prison was simple when he put it together: Like any adversity, prison can make and break a person, the type of making and breaking depends entirely on how the person spends their time and views their predicament.

As far as the people that left him, he chalked it up to him not giving them enough to love about him to want to stay. He knows he didn't make a big enough impact in their lives to keep himself relevant. So he didn't become bitter or angry, he accepted things the way they were, but he vowed to make a change and start making an impact on the new people that entered his life so they would never leave him. Jason spent his time learning: learning how to express himself eloquently, which led to him writing poetry that was quite good and was often published in the prison's monthly newsletters.

He got involved in ancient history and philosophy and he studied several religions and spiritualities. He didn't consider himself religious, just in-tune with himself and his place in creation. He would often talk to other prisoners about the things he learned because he felt it was his duty to enlighten those who didn't know, but wanted to. But there was a slight problem Jason was having—he felt like he was becoming socially reclusive. He had no problems talking to other prisoners but when it came to people outside of the world in which he now lived, he found it difficult to initiate a conversation on even the most frivolous of topics.

Before he got locked up he never had an issue with approaching women, in fact, it came naturally; since then he's become reserved and standoffish—even shy. In his mind he rationalizes it by saying the women here have no interest in him beyond what their job requires and when they act like they do it's a trap, an ego game they play to see the reaction they can get out of men.

All of this has made him question his confidence and self-worth. He's seen a few female guards over the years he would actually be interested in—even on the streets—but none have affected him more than Jenny Berberick but he hasn't been able to build the courage up to at least hint his attraction towards her. He tells himself the timing hasn't been right or when he does get ready she isn't working that day, so he does the only thing he knows how: he dreams about her. But even in his dreams he can't seem to solidify something entirely real with her.

He got up and washed his face, shaved and brushed his teeth. By the time he finished dressing it was 6:45a.m. He turned his T.V. on and waited for the cell doors to be opened for breakfast. This has been his routine for many years now and he looked forward to it because every new day brought him closer to freedom. He was one of the swampers in Cell Hall C so he got let out fifteen minutes before the rest of the unit. His job was to collect all of the trash, bag it up, set it in the hall in the morning and then before lunch he swept and mopped the floors—one of the easiest jobs in the joint and he got a dollar an hour for his troubles. He began his job and quickly, but subtly, did a staff check to see if Jenny was working—she wasn't. Well, maybe she's working later, he thought.

Later that morning he went outside to walk the yard and think; he saw his buddy, Old man Leon, sitting at one of the tables.

"Mornin' Jason," he said in his old whisper of a voice.

"Hey Leon, how's it going?" Jason responded as he took a seat across from the old man.

"Not bad. It's a nice day out here. I had to come enjoy it while it last; I don't know how many more days I got left in me anyway."

"Aww, stop that Leon, you're probably gonna outlive me."

"Who says I want to?" he asked with a faraway look in his rheumy eyes. "I've seen too many people I know go before me already—I don't wanna see any more."

Leon was what prisoners called an "Old Timer"; he's been in prison for almost forty years. His story was truly a tragic one. He came home from drinking with some friends one night and found his wife in bed with another man. He shot his wife with a hunting rifle and made the guy run out of the house butt naked.

As he went to call the police to tell them what he did he heard the guy come back in the room so he turned around and shot him. But it turned out to be his ten year old son who woke up from the noise. He was going to shoot himself but he couldn't find any more bullets. Jason didn't judge him though; since he met the man seven years ago he's been nothing but a good friend.

"So anyhow," he quickly changed the subject, "have you thought anymore about what I told you last week?"

"Yeah," he started a little hesitantly, "but as much as I want to believe you, my mind is telling me that it's impossible."

"That's the problem with you youngsters today—your minds are closed. You've gotta open your mind up to other possibilities; even the ones that seem impossible. Remember, we're dealing with the mind here; nothing is impossible."

"So you're telling me if I focus hard enough in my dreams I can bring them to life?" Jason asked pensively.

"No son. I'm telling you that your dreams are alive already, you just have to find the key to animate them in this realm!" Leon had an intensity burning in his eyes now; a clarity that only seemed to show itself when he talked about dreams.

"How do I find the key? Where do I start looking?" He wanted that key so bad because he knew he could make a great impact on the world and… he could get Jenny to notice him.

"Find the key…" the old man said as if coming back from somewhere else, "not everybody is meant to find the key. Some people—most people—go through life never giving dreams a second thought. Why? Because their minds aren't ready to accept its reality!" Leon paused while Jason eagerly waited for the old man to continue.

"You're familiar with myths and parables right?"

"Yeah, of course."

"Well, you and I know that the Jesus Myth, the Osiris Myth are stories that encode a culture's beliefs, customs, views on morality and virtues. They get lost in translation when they're literalized, the message gets distorted and instead of focusing on the lessons people get caught up in picking sides as a 'believer' or a 'non-believer.' A dream is a personal myth and religion is the world's dream!"

"How do you know so much about this Leon?"

"I've been around a long time and I've learned that listening is better than talking, most times. Listening doesn't just mean opening your ears up to everything you hear, though. Listening means being receptive to everything of value, hearing it in all its many forms, whether they be written words, spoken words or no words at all—silence—watching the things around you and picking up the lessons talking within its movements or structure."

There were times when Jason thought the old man was crazy but when he talked like this, he knew Leon was a wise man and far from crazy.

"So did you order that book from the county library?" Leon asked.

"Yeah, I put in the slip last Tuesday."

"It should be here today then. Jung's going to give you some deeper insight; he dealt with a lot of dream psychology. Let me know if you find something useful."

"I definitely will," Jason assured him.

"You're almost out the door huh; you got an immediate plan besides the long term goals you've already told me about?"

"Well, I don't have any family that I know of and I don't want to live with anybody right away, so I'll be going to a half-way house until I get myself situated. I've been working with this prisoner's release program for the past four months and they said they'll have a job or at least some very good leads for me soon after I get out."

"Jason you're a sharp guy; sharper than anyone I've ever met your age. Make sure you do the right thing and practice what you've been preaching around here. Don't come back."

"I—"

"THE YARD IS CLOSED. RETURN TO YOUR UNITS!" Came over the loudspeaker, letting prisoners know they were still on prison time.

"Alright Leon, you take it easy."

"I'm gonna take it how it's given—anything else is rape."

Jason had a good laugh at that. Leon's old convict humor never got old to him.

"I'll be out here tomorrow old man."

"See ya then youngster."

With that they both headed to their respective units. After going to the gym, Jason showered and got ready to go to the library. When he got to the library and asked about the book he requested from the county library the librarian informed him that the book request was denied because he has less than four months left. Instead of leaving right away he went to the new arrivals section, found something of interest, checked it out and went back to his cell hall. He stayed in his cell reading the rest of the night.

The next two weeks were pretty much the same thing as prison life tends to be. The only difference was these two weeks were the longest of his entire life; they say it's always like that at the end. He had three days to go and he would be a free man again. Jason didn't have the jitters he'd seen a lot of guys get when their out date approached, none of the erratic behaviors and telltale signs that he would be coming back or getting himself killed shortly after his release. No, he was ready.

Things were looking good for him, especially since officer Berberick was on closet duty when he got ready to put away the clean uniforms.

"Hey Berberick?" he said as he approached her post, ignoring the other officer sitting there with her.

"What's up Madison?"

"Can you open the closet so I can put away the uniforms, please?"

"Sure can," she said as she got up and headed towards the closet. As they closed the short distance to the closet he asked her how her day was going. She told him there were no fights or reports to write so it was going good so far. She returned the question and told him she heard he was getting out real soon. He told her everything was looking good and he only had three days left. She smiled, looking genuinely happy for him as she opened the closet and stepped to the side to let him in the with the uniforms.

"Are you nervous?" she asked him.

"Nah, I'm too focused to be nervous. I'm just eager to get back out there and live—really live—'cause this right here isn't living."

"You sound like you've learned your lesson," she said seriously.

"Oh, I have. This was my first and last time."

"I hope it is. You don't fit in here. I mean that as a compliment," she added quickly when he cocked an eyebrow up at her.

"I'm glad you can see that. Thank you for the compliment," he said, feeling a bit of déjà vu. He was done stacking the uniforms, but he wanted to keep talking; he might not ever get this opportunity again. He turned towards her and took his shot.

"Maybe I could thank you with lunch someday," he said as he looked directly in her eyes. His heart was beating fast and he was sure a reprimand was on its way—oh well, at least he tried. He didn't say anything perverted; he just offered to buy her lunch. If he had to do his last two days in the hole for that—so be it. All of this ran through his mind as he steeled himself for her response. She smiled and said maybe.

He stepped out of the closet, lightly brushing past her and said he'd hold her to that.

She locked the door and returned to her post without another word.

Jason walked back to his cell and prepared to go outside to see Leon for the last time as his fellow inmate. He couldn't help being a little paranoid, thinking officer Berberick was writing an incident report right now, with the security response team waiting for him outside his cell. But none of the above seemed to be transpiring as he shut his cell and headed for the metal detectors. He found old man Leon sitting at his usual table and joined him.

"What's up old man? How are you?"

"Another day I'm still in control of my bowels so I'm pretty good," he said with not a hint of humor.

"I guess that's a good way to look at it," Jason replied with a chuckle.

"Damn right it is." He paused and then grew serious as he spoke. "Listen Jason, you've been given a second chance and there's no doubt in my mind you're gonna take advantage of it." Leon reached across the table and slid him a perfectly folded piece of paper the size of a silver dollar, known as a "kite" in the joint.

"That should get you set up right away," he said as Jason pocketed the kite. "I've been down 37 years; seen many come and go and come right back. This isn't a life for anyone, although some of these knuckleheads need this structure 'cause they don't know how to control themselves. But, you... I've seen you grow over the past seven years. You've got something the world needs a lot more of. Do something with it, youngster, please."

"I don't feel like I have any other choice, Leon," he said sincerely, matching the old man's seriousness. "I've gotta make it and for me that means more than just staying out, it means having something worthy to offer and offering it up every chance I get." They sat silent for a minute or so until Jason asked Leon if he needed him to do anything for him when he got out.

"Nah, I've got enough money to last until they bury me in here and I don't have any family—"

"Yeah you do Leon," Jason cut it.

"Don't go makin' any promises, I'm not asking you to do anything for me," the old man cautioned.

"I'm not promising anything, I'm just stating a fact old man — you're not alone anymore. Let's just leave it at that," he said sternly.

"Now when you get out there make sure you get on that internet thing," Leon went on, glad to change the subject, "You should be able to find a lot of information on this dream stuff."

"Oh, that's one of my top priorities —"

"THE YARD IS CLOSED. REPORT TO YOUR UNITS!"

Leon stood up, walked over to Jason and stuck his hand out. Jason shook it, and then embraced the old man.

"I'll send you all my info as soon as I get settled," Jason said.

"You take care of yourself out there son."

"I will Leon."

As Leon headed back to his unit, Jason watched him through teary eyes and noticed with pride and warmth that the old man walked a little straighter, head held a little higher.

CHAPTER 4

The findings are quite remarkable, Semi!" the biochemist said excitedly. "As you know there are two primary forms of melanin: neuromelanin or the grey matter of the brain and surface melanin which deals with the coloring of skin and hair and varies from race to race and even varies within the same gene pool. Most neuroscientists completely ignore surface melanin and focus their studies on the light-sensitive neuromelanin found in the spinal line, brain stem and nervous system of all higher forms of life; and rightly so I would say."

Semi, who was paying close attention, but didn't appear to be due to his lack of any facial expression, raised his eyebrows slightly from where he sat, indicating that the biochemist should continue. Dr. Reese Jackson is a large effusive man with large jowls that droop slightly so it gives him a look of always being on the verge of tears, except when he smiles, which he does a lot... then he looks like a giant Care Bear. His plump, sad face is offset by his indomitable chipper attitude. He cleared his throat and continued.

"The only time surface melanin gets any real attention is in those cases of skin cancer, you know melanoma and such, which is really a shame. Anyway, as we began testing skin and hair samples, isolating and extracting the melanin from it so we could concentrate it, somehow, there was a mix-up, a rather fortunate one, I must admit. Surface melanin from a black male was mixed with a sample of highly concentrated neuromelanin. It wasn't immediately noticed until… Well, here, I think you should see this for yourself."

Semi is a tall and wiry man who is deceptively strong and agile. He has ebony skin, a low-cut hairstyle and a smooth hairless face that gives him a much younger appearance than his forty-nine years. With his piercing light-brown eyes, strong features and West Indian accent, he's the quintessence of an African Adonis.

Semi slowly stood and followed Dr. Jackson to a table where labeled petri dishes and microscope slides and vials rested in an incubator, the size and shape of a small refrigerator. Next to the incubator were several high powered microscopes and a highly advanced computer. The rotund biochemist grabbed a dish, removed the thin lid that covered the drop of melanin that was no bigger than half the size of a raindrop and placed it under a high powered electron microscope. The melanin was so dark, so black it looked as if there was an empty space; a hole in the center of the petri dish that went all the way through the bottom of the microscope's holding tray and right through the table.

The biochemist made some adjustments on the microscope and then moved his robust frame aside while gesturing for Semi to take a look. He asked Semi what he saw when he looked through the microscope's lens and then back up at him.

"It's moving… undulating like a microscopic body of water," Semi replied, not hiding his intrigue.

"Precisely, it's reacting to the light. Remember, neuromelanin is light-sensitive. Now look at this." Dr. Jackson removed the dish, covered it and put it back into the incubator. He then took another petri dish and placed it under the microscope and motioned for Semi to look again.

"This one is not moving at all," Semi said.

"This is the European male sample; it's completely fallow," he paused and then enticingly added, "without stimulation that is."

Semi patiently asked him what he meant, but Dr. Jackson was already in motion, preparing to show him. He reached under the table and pulled a small electronic device from a drawer and plugged it into the microscope; he fidgeted with it then stepped back. Semi, taking that as a sign the scientist wanted him to look through the microscope again, started to do just that.

"No, wait!" Dr. Jackson said quickly.

Semi stopped and looked at the large man with his piercing stare.

"Sorry, but that would've been bad. Very bad. I'll explain in a moment, you'll be able to—" The tiny dot of neuromelanin began pulsating a dark light, an unearthly glow that reminded Semi of looking into outer space with a telescope.

Dr. Jackson explained that the machine he just plugged into the microscope is called a Brain Wave Simulator—which he and the other scientist call "The Brain"—and it emits the same electrical charge as the human brain: about 25 watts. He then told Semi that nerve signals move at over 270mph without conscious effort, while awake, but a dreaming brain's synaptic process moves at a much higher rate. Somewhere between three and four hundred mph; subsequently the electrical impulse of the brain elevates and this is a crucial part of The Brain's function.

Dr. Jackson pressed a button on The Brain and the dot of melanin began glowing darker. He told Semi not to focus directly on the melanin, but to look at the petri dish it's in. Semi took his eyes away from the glowing dot and let his gaze wander to the dish it was resting in.

"Where'd the petri dish go?" he asked, not hiding his bafflement. The area that should've been the dish was now the same unearthly blackness as the melanin, looking as if it was growing and consuming everything. The only difference was the glowing, dark—light was only coming from the center where the actual sample was. The area was so dark it looked as if a black hole was forming, making the surrounding light seem dimmer while casting its own dark luminosity.

"It's still there!" Dr. Jackson said excitedly, "the melanin has just caused its immediate surroundings to imitate it! The potential implications are astounding, to say the least."

Semi's thoughts were already there; thinking of what this could mean and how he could use it to his advantage once it was fully understood.

"Now the black male sample has the same reaction externally but we believe an internal reaction would yield different results; we haven't tested that. What's even more astonishing, however, is the chemical composition has radically changed. You are now seeing the elusive DimethylTryptamine, also known as DMT! We have virtually replicated the same process that occurs during vitamin D synthesis, when the skin is exposed to ultraviolet rays from sunlight." Semi's eyes widened and he looked at the sample with greater appreciation. "However, it is not very potent, but we believe the higher the concentration the more potent the DMT will be. But it's costly too; this sample here was developed at the expense of an entire patient."

"Don't concern yourself with the cost, Reese, it will be paid one way or another and patients will continue to be available. In the meantime I want you to get the potency right and start—"

"Manufacturing DMT?" Dr. Jackson cut in with a smile. "I've already begun working on the formula," he finished as he glanced fondly at the glowing DMT/Melanin.

"Good, very good," Semi replied approvingly. Finally, years of research and tens of thousands of dollars spent would pay off. The prospect of producing DMT on a large scale did more for Semi than the biochemist knew. Of course the class 1 illegal psychedelic drug would bring in a lot of money, seeing as entheogens have become as popular as acid was in the 1960s, but Semi had other plans for it as well; plans Dr. Jackson would surely scoff at.

There was no problem believing in a hallucinogen that could alter the state of consciousness, after all, melatonin, the sleep hormone does just that—putting waking consciousness to sleep while the body still operates normally. But, one that claimed to transport the user to a parallel reality and/or allow them access to the collective consciousness with the ability to change reality through it, well… that was a hard pill for the scientific community to swallow.

Semi knew better, though. Shamans, monks, and mystics have been doing that for thousands of years through various herbal mixtures, mental disciplines and meditation techniques that take many, many years of training to master. He hoped this new compound would accelerate the process.

Dr. Jackson went on explaining and Semi knew the doctor enjoyed being able to talk it out because it helped him process the information better himself. So he always humored him.

"DMT is created by many organs in the body: the retina, lungs, thyroid gland et cetera, but once it enters the bloodstream it is destroyed immediately, by a chemical called Monoamine Oxidase—MAO; this is why it can't be accurately detected by a blood test. Now here's where it gets really interesting. The pineal gland is known to contain the most serotonin rich tissue in the body and it's widely believed that it must also contain the richest source of DMT as well, since DMT is actually serotonin with two methyl groups attached to it—created after the pineal gland secretes an enzyme called Methyltransferase. We have been able to give some credence to that theory due to our, um… unrestricted access to the patients. The thing is, the production of this DMT must be triggered—that trigger is brain stimulation and a mixture of concentrated surface and neuromelanin."

"But, wouldn't the MAO still attack and destroy it?" Semi asked, clearly following along. Dr. Jackson smiled so wide his cheeks formed two mountains that lifted his glasses from the bridge of his nose briefly.

"Yes, that's exactly what we were expecting until we realized the compound is not in the bloodstream, or the body at all for that matter; it was created in a petri dish so exposure to MAO never happened!" Semi was already nodding his head in understanding.

"Why did you tell me not to look at the sample through the microscope once you plugged in the Brain Wave Simulator?"

"Oh, because you would've been blinded. Permanently." Dr. Jackson said matter-of-factly. "Your pupils would have been completely filled with an impenetrable darkness and—"

"How is that, when only one of my eyes would've been exposed?" Semi interjected, looking at the single-lens microscope.

"Well, it's simple actually: you would've looked through the microscope with your right eye and once you thought you couldn't see anything, you would've tried again with your left eye. That's why we're using single-lens microscopes." Semi smiled mirthlessly; a smile that everyone who has ever seen found unsettling—despite his handsome face. Dr. Jackson swallowed and continued.

"Smith was the first to lose his sight. Stevenson figured it out after he too looked at the charged sample. As of right now we haven't figured out why the naked eye is unaffected, but the consensus is that the charged melanin is amplified enough through the microscope, so that it does the same things that—"

"It causes its surroundings—in this case the eyes—to imitate it. That is very intriguing indeed. Figure out how to harness that and recreate it on a bigger scale," Semi finished.

"You mean like a weapon?"

"I like to think of it more like a tool but, yes you can call it a weapon. And that," he nodded towards the still-glowing sample of neuromelanin/DMT, "give it top priority and keep me updated on any new developments."

Dr. Jackson nodded and began shutting down the microscope and the Brainwave Simulator. When he returned the now normal looking sample of neuromelanin to the incubator he spoke again. "Uh, Semi, can we see about getting Smith's and Stevenson's eyesight restored? I know a great opthamologist, and Stevenson has been a serious asset to the research."

"Yes, Stevenson is a very adept biologist and I know we would do well to have him able-bodied and working. Contact your ophthalmologist," Semi replied. He would be foolish not to find out if the blindness was permanent or able to be reversed; especially since he planned on weaponizing it and he truly did value Stevenson.

"And Smith" Dr. Jackson asked hopefully and tugged at his huge lab coat.

"Dr. Smith has made a great sacrifice in the name of science, and his contributions have definitely benefited our research." Dr. Jackson sighed inwardly, relieved that Semi would help both men regain their vision. The three of them worked very well together.

"However, his services are no longer needed." Semi finished succinctly. Dr. Jackson's shoulders slumped, like a disappointed child begging to have a friend sleep over but being told no with unyielding finality. Semi never hid his disdain for the arrogant physicist and was always close to "letting him go." He only tolerated him because he was undeniably brilliant; the most capable of the fifteen scientists he employed. He would find another.

Being well aware of Smith and Semi's tenuous relationship, Dr. Jackson knew there would be no persuading him, so he wisely decided not to press the issue. He wasn't too put off by Semi's decision; they were all paid very well and informed from the beginning that the terms of their employment included accepting some on-the-job hazards. That, and Reese Jackson was now head of the research team. At least he wasn't going to have Smith disappear. With that final thought, Dr. Jackson thrust thoughts of Smith from his mind.

"Come, let's have a look at our donors," Semi said and flashed a disarming smile. They walked down the center aisle of the lab, passing several other scientists who were working diligently on related projects at island-style workstations. Some sat in front of computers, oblivious to anything other than the data they were reviewing and entering into the system. Some had various rodents, conducting experiments with the enthusiasm of a kid who just figured out that he could burn ants with a magnifying glass. And others huddled around microscopes, examining samples in petri dishes and slides.

All of them were engrossed in their work, and Semi knew all were capable of making a monumental breakthrough at any moment. They are the best in their fields—biologists, biochemists, physicists and other ologists he's never heard of. They were shunned by mainstream academics; considered pariahs because they're willing to do the experiments most call perverse and unethical, and wouldn't dare do under the most careful circumstances.

Recruiting was easy. One man's trash is another man's treasure, as the saying goes, Semi thought sardonically. These are some of the best minds in the world and could, no doubt, aid in the advancement of civilization; but those in power are too soft and weak-minded to make the necessary sacrifices; they let their self-righteousness and moral probity stagnate the progress of the human race. Semion Djaneve would not let such things get in the way.

The two men stopped at a thick, windowless metal door with a camera pointing down at them. Dr. Jackson produced a key and inserted it into the lock and they entered a prison-like foyer of plain white brick walls, reinforced with thick steel and a door heavier than the first one. Semi smiled to himself. He knew this underground structure could easily hold off a military assault, if it ever came to that.

When the outer door closed, both men put their right hands in what appeared to be palm-scanners, placed on opposite sides of the inner door. These were no ordinary palm-scanners, however. They did not read the finger or the palm prints of a hand; instead the state-of-the-art biometrics system worked through sophisticated vein pattern recognition technology. Regular palm and retina scanners were good, but they had a major flaw: they could not detect whether the hand or eye it was scanning was attached to the person. VPR technology could not only verify that the person's extremity was attached, but by monitoring the vital signs and the subtle contractions of the veins as blood was pumped through, could accurately detect signs of distress and therefore deny entry based on any irregularity.

Seconds later the thundering clap of the heavy locking mechanism releasing sounded in the small confines, causing Dr. Jackson to jump and then look at Semi sheepishly. No matter how many times he's been through the process it still catches him off guard. Semi ignored him and pushed the heavy door open.

The room they entered had the antiseptic feel of a hospital, with its spotless white floors, walls, and bright overhead fluorescent lighting. But that is where the similarities ended. That hospital feel was overshadowed by the high-tech gadgets that occupied every countertop and corner in the room. The two rows of five Stasis machines at the very back made Semion feel like he just boarded a spaceship that was in a hangar bay, preparing for deep space travel.

The three doctors in the room acknowledged the two men's presence with the cursory glances of professionals too busy to bother with any niceties. And that was okay with Semi, for he did not acknowledge them at all; he knew they were there and would call on them if he needed them.

As he made his way to the back of the room, his focus was on the tube-like vessels where the donors rested. These six-foot machines resembled tanning beds in size, but were completely enclosed and hermetically sealed when activated. The rounded surface of the outer shell looked a lot like tinted glass, allowing anyone on the outside a full view of the person inside. What made the glass unique, however, is it doesn't allow any light to penetrate the inside, so that if the occupant was conscious they would be in absolute darkness. That would not bother the current occupants though, because they believed they were involved in a study, testing the effects of total darkness and silence on REM sleep.

They had no clue they were suspended in stasis and kept alive by a thick viscous fluid called Liquid Nano-Technology, which supplied them with oxygen and all the essential nutrients needed to sustain human life; even waste elimination was handled by the Liquid Nanos. The blue liquid had more of a jelly-like consistency and its color resembled that of Windex with millions of tiny white particles floating throughout it; though appeared to be clear when seen through the Stasis machines.

Dr. Jackson and Semi reached the first row and stopped at the first machine's terminal. Along with holding each patient's medical information, the terminal monitored vital signs, controlled the climate, and every function necessary for research and assessments. Dr. Jackson entered his passcode and began pulling up the patient's medical file for Semi to view.

"This is who I was referring to when I mentioned the anomaly during our conversation this morning," Dr. Jackson said as he continued to rapidly press the touch screen and talk almost as fast. "Now you have to understand Semi, I had no idea what we were dealing with; the guys bring them in and then they're cleaned and immediately placed in the Stasis machines, so we can conduct the medical background check."

Liquid Nano Technology is a solution developed in the early 2000s by the Mayo Clinic's Sports Medicine Center as a regenerative therapy treatment; helping athletes heal on a molecular level. It quickly drew the attention of other scientists and advanced to become used for numerous procedures, like reversing once-irreversible cases of frostbite, to almost entirely eliminating the risks during complicated neurosurgeries. However, it only works in conjunction with the Stasis machines, which are very expensive to operate and therefore inaccessible to most people. Semi, being a co-inventor, didn't have to worry about the expense.

"It seems no one thought it important to inform me that we had our first female patient. We already had her processed and through the preliminary tests, so I decided to proceed with the melanin analysis; I figured it wouldn't hurt to compare her levels. After I had her levels I would've had her released of course," Dr. Jackson rambled.

Semion peered into the now clear, thick glass of the Stasis machine and looked at the serene female face that lay within. She was as dark as he was and innocently youthful looking. A bit too youthful, he thought as his piercing eyes scanned over the length of her exposed body.

"Reese," Semi cut in with extreme calm, "the anomaly?"

"Oh, yes, yes! Well, you see, this female's neuromelanin analysis shows a fifty percent higher concentration than all the male samples we have… combined!"

Although he showed little emotion on his face, the gears were turning and something very close to excitement was budding.

"And… you let her being a female stop you from beginning the extraction process?" Semi asked.

"Well, no, it's her age… she's twelve years old," Dr. Jackson said dejectedly. Seeing this most intriguing scientific opportunity slip away, his fervor waned and his cheeks drooped as he further explained himself. "We didn't know until the Nanos worked their way through her system and I completely reviewed the results. She, uh, doesn't have—she doesn't look twelve, so I can see how one of the guys may have made a mistake." He fell silent as he awaited the rebuke and reprimand that was sure to come in that deadly composed demeanor he found far more unsettling than a loud and animated rant.

Semion Djaneve clasped his hands behind his back and studied the girl more intently. When he spoke it was as if he was solving a riddle.

"You must change and become like little children. If you don't, you will never enter the kingdom of heaven."

"Huh?" Dr. Jackson said.

"Matthew 18:3. Tell me, doctor, exactly what the anomaly is."

"Of course; you see it is widely accepted as fact that while surface Melanin may differ in its concentration, neuromelanin or the grey matter is pretty much the same in everyone. What that means is the level of neurotransmitters and neurons are the same, though the volume may be concentrated at different locations in the brain. The thing is we can only extrapolate right now because we have no female data and as far as I know, no one has been able to examine children's brains so closely. So we don't know if it's her being a female or being a child that gives her stronger neuromelanin."

"So many questions… It's about time we got some answers. Wouldn't you agree, doc?"

"Yes, it would be a remarkable opportunity," Dr. Jackson eagerly agreed. Semi made his way to the control command terminal that could control and override all or as many of the machines as the operator chose.

"Then we must make some room." He selected an option on the screen and immediately a low humming noise sounded. An almost imperceptible vibration could be felt through the floor as the Liquid Nano solution from nine stasis machines was drained and routed through the convoluted pipe system to be recycled.

"But, but we could still…" Dr. Jackson stammered. As the last of the Nanos left the interior of the machines, the occupants began to regain consciousness—unfortunately, because along with the solution went their oxygen.

Nine men of different colors, ages, and backgrounds began struggling for a breath that would never come again. Dr. Jackson looked on uncomfortably as some pounded or scratched at the impenetrable glass, seeking a way out of the enclosure that once sustained their lives, but was now taking them. One guy didn't resist at all, he calmly laid there and seemed to welcome his demise. His only movement was the final death spasms as his body gave in to the deprivation of oxygen. In the end, nine bodies that were alive just minutes ago lay still; eyes slightly bulged and united by similar faces of death. Dr. Jackson removed his glasses with a tremulous, meaty hand and wiped beads of sweat from his face with the sleeve of his lab coat.

"We all must make sacrifices for the advancement of humanity—these men made the ultimate sacrifice. We've found what we have been in search of and now, the real work, the hard work begins," Semi elevated his voice so the other doctors could hear him. They had all halted what they were doing as soon as they understood what had just happened.

"You all," he pointed at them, "have been given the opportunity to change the world with the research you are engaged in, but everything has a price. Those not willing to pay it or those who don't have what it takes to see the price paid by others should walk away now." He paused and looked each person in the eye. No one flinched.

He nodded his approval, pointed at the one remaining living occupant in the stasis machine and when he spoke, it was with passionate conviction. "We shall show the world that the stars can be reached here on earth… and she will lead the way."

CHAPTER 5

Tony McNeil never made it to school that next week or the week after, and he hasn't seen his best friend in over four years. Almost immediately after his siblings were buried his mother got sick. It was an emotional sickness that drained her spirit and sparked the complete depletion of her moxie. She quickly spiraled down to the depths of despondency and that depression soon manifested itself physically. So he became responsible for the maintenance of the entire household, and his mom.

The morning after the last night she visited Thomas in the hospital, as he lay in a coma, Tony went into his mother's room to tell her about a bill collector but she acted like she didn't hear him because she didn't stir where she lay under the covers. When he shook her and pulled the covers back, it was clear she had been dead for a few hours. She overdosed on pain pills.

Once again, Tony's life changed. The only family he knew of was his mom's mother and she never hid the fact that she only had room for Lisa in her heart—Tony and Tommy didn't exist to her. After his brother and sister died his mother and grandmother got into a huge fight because his grandmother pressed his mom for years to let Lisa live with her, and she said, quite viciously, Lisa would still be here if she would've listened to her.

The ensuing years were a blur as he went from one shelter to another and from school to school. The fact that he couldn't save his family with his dreams made him discard and ignore his ability like a useless notion. Neith made her presence felt throughout the years, so despite his perpetually dismal circumstances, he never felt completely alone.

When he turned thirteen, he ended up at Grover Homes, a group home for teens. It was at the other end of the state but it seemed like a world away. Tony had another gift, though: resiliency. His ability to focus on the good and not the bad allowed him to make the most out of his situation. One good thing is Grover Homes has the biggest library he has ever seen right next to it, and as a resident, he gets full access. His voraciousness for reading and his precocity were quickly noticed, so he and the librarian naturally hit it off.

Grover Homes consisted of four cottages: one for boys, one for girls, the main cottage, and the school cottage. The main cottage was the biggest; it had the intake offices where new arrivals were processed, the large dining hall where both resident cottages came to eat main meals; a health services department and a recreational area that had a few old computers, board games, TVs, and vending machines.

The school was actually very much like a normal one, albeit smaller, but it offered the same curriculum and even had a small gym. The library was across from the school but it wasn't an official part of Grover Homes. The director offered its services to the school after a city meeting for funding didn't get the necessary votes. Council members cited the recent financial crisis as the reason, but everyone knew they just didn't care enough. There wasn't much resistance because the majority of the kids there have no outside representatives to push for them

For Tony, though, the living conditions weren't all that bad. The room he shared with two other boys reminded him of his old room; it was bigger but it had the same feel. The furnishings were sparse, which probably made the room feel bigger than it actually was. Tony's single bed stood opposite his two roommates' bunk bed against off white walls. Faux oak dressers rested against the back walls and under the beds each boy had a trunk for additional storage. A single table stood in the middle of the back wall, under the room's only window. The room was lit by a ceiling fan and light fixture, which made the thin blue carpet look cleaner than it was.

"Listen Mark, I told you: you can't win. You're too outta shape." Javontay stated with unwavering confidence.

"Man, how many times do I have to tell you, it's Marcus. And just because I got a few extra pounds on me doesn't mean I'm outta shape," Marcus replied with equal confidence.

"A few extra pounds," Tay said over-dramatically, "boy Doritos get lost in your fat folds when you drop 'em on your stomach."

Tony suppressed a laugh as he sat at the table with his back against the window, studying a book. "So, I always find them... eventually. Man, you're stalling with those stale jokes," Marcus said, not the least bit bothered by the jab.

"The only thing stale is those Doritos you find somewhere on your belly a week later."

Tony didn't even try to hold it this time. He erupted into a hearty laugh. When he stopped, he put a bookmark in his book and closed it. He wouldn't be getting any further with these two in the room. "Alright, you got me with that, but you know you're stalling Tay. Tony, come watch this so he can't say I cheated somehow... or he slipped."

Tony got up and positioned himself by the door and watched as the other two got in the middle of the room, circling each other, waiting to make their move.

Javontay lunged at Marcus's upper body, wrapping muscular arms around him, thinking to simply muscle the chubby teen to the ground. With surprising swiftness, Marcus dropped from Javontay's grasp, grabbed his waist and then used his right heel to sweep Tay's left leg while he brought all his weight down. Both of them went down but Marcus was on top, and in control.

"Point!" Tony called out.

"Man, hold on; I wasn't ready. Run it back," Tay said as the two of them scrambled to their feet.

"Last one. We gotta hit the showers before lights out," Tony said.

Marcus and Tay squared off again, stalking each other, waiting for an opening. This time Javontay took the time to assess his opponent. He knows he's taller, stronger, and more agile, but Marcus is shorter and quicker. Maybe his height was working against him… he got low, squatting in a football stance, but when he went to charge, he hit nothing but air. Marcus, anticipating the jock, sidestepped him and circled low so when Tay turned around he was already under him and taking out his legs.

"Match! Marcus won," Tony said in his best officiating voice.

Marcus stood up while Tay lay there, looking dumbfounded.

"You underestimated me," Marcus said, "That's why you lost." He extended his hand. Tay took it and pulled himself up.

"Damn dude, I definitely didn't think you could move that fast," Tay said with admiration.

"Never judge a book by its cover," Marcus said, "like Tony always says."

"Or the first couple chapters; you suck at football *and* basketball so I thought for sure you had no chance at wrestling!" Javontay said as he shook his hand with humility.

"Lights out in twenty-five minutes; I'm taking a shower. You two should do the same—y'all are funky."

"That's those stale Doritos," Tay said. All three of them cracked up as they gathered their shower gear and headed for the washrooms.

Later that night as they lay in their beds, Tony thought about his two roommates. It's weird how a situation like theirs can bring together three diametric personalities that in high school or any other normal circumstances would have them at odds with each other. Javontay Williams, a seventeen year old superstar-athlete in training, was not your typical high school meathead jock. What made him different was under all that toughness and competitive drive, he had good character; he never bullied anyone and he was smart. He had his shortcomings and secrets, but everyone here does. After losing his father to the prison system and his mother to drugs, he ended up in Grover Homes. He had the kind of charisma that made him popular quick: confident, witty, and kind. But he didn't revel in it; he seemed to want to avoid his popularity, which was pretty easy when he started hanging out with the two he now shared a room with.

Marcus Filborn, a seventeen-year-old mixed kid who was a little on the heavy side but definitely no slouch, was not only a class clown, but also the butt of the class clown's jokes. He took it all in stride, though, being the self-deprecating type. That's what made him so likable to a lot of the kids here. But under that humor was a repressed anger and pain that only Tony seemed to pick up on. His mother died when he was five. He was raised by an abusive dad who verbally abused him and beat him without mercy for big things like oversleeping and being too lazy. He came to school with so many bruises one day that a teacher saw them and reported them. When child protection questioned his dad, he didn't even deny the beatings, he simply said "I raise that boy the best I can—hell, I took worse beatings when I was younger than him." He was placed in Grover Homes shortly after.

Tony was pretty much invisible in the group home. He stayed to himself and out of everyone else's way. He was known as the bookworm and sometimes the genius, but never the nerd or geek. His first day at Grover Homes, he met Marcus who was getting bullied by two older kids. Tony didn't like fighting and he avoided it as much as he could, but even before he became a ward of the state, he was no stranger to having to defend himself. When the two bullies jumped on Marcus, Tony didn't hesitate to throw himself in to even things out. He and Marcus got beat up, but they got their respect as well, and more than that, they became friends.

"So what's up with you and Jamesha, Tay?" Marcus asked, snapping through Tony's musing. "Man, she's all over you."

"Aren't all the girls, though?" Tony said dryly.

"Nah, just a couple," Tay modestly replied, "out of all of them, though, I do like Jamesha the most. She just seems more mature—"

"Yeah, with a booty like that, I bet she is a lot more mature," Marcus cut in.

"Yes, she does have a nice body," Tay said with admiration, "but, I mean, she doesn't drool all over me like the others. You know?"

"Sure. I know." Marcus said and snorted derisively.

"She lets me know that she likes me, but she doesn't chase me; she makes me chase her. I think that's what makes me like her even more," Tay finished.

"I see what you're saying. Those other girls are like McDonalds and Jamesha is a home cooked meal by grandma—yeah, I get it."

"Boy, how do you make everything about food?!" Tay said with humorous exasperation.

"Shoot, I love food," Marcus responded innocently, as he fumbled with the wrapper of a midnight snack.

"That was a good analogy, though," Tony said with a chuckle from across the room on his single bed. Javontay jumped back in, asking Marcus what the deal was with him and Teresa. He knew he liked her. And Marcus readily admitted that he did, around a mouthful of something sweet.

"You gotta talk to her then; let her know you're feelin' her."

"It's not that easy man."

"Uh, yeah it is. You can laugh and joke all day with girls but you can't let one know you like her? Come on man."

"I'll let her know when I'm ready; when the time is right… you gotta let the chicken get golden brown before you take it out the grease."

"That was another good one," Tony chimed in, "and he's right; you have to let him do it when he's ready or he might mess up."

"Right, right… like you do huh?" Tay said sarcastically. Tony innocently asked Tay what he was talking about because for all his book smarts, he didn't have much experience on this subject.

"When are you going to be ready for Ashley, or Brianna, 'cause both of them have been giving you that you-can-get-it look for a long time now and I bet you've never noticed?"

"I talk to both of them all the time," Tony said matter-of-factly.

"And what do y'all talk about? Schoolwork, books, and boring stuff like that," Tay answered himself, "you gotta read between the lines. They're just using the school work and books as an excuse to be around you!" Tay finished, sounding like an exasperated teacher. Marcus cut in and asked Tony which girl he liked the most. Tony said Ashley, with an exaggerated sigh.

"Good choice," Marcus replied.

"Okay, cool," Tay jumped in, sounding like a coach as he leaned over his bunk and started moving his hands like he was directing a play. "This is what I'm a do. I'm a set something up for all of us tomorrow—" Tony and Marcus began to protest. " Listen, just hear me out. It's not like I'm asking y'all to kiss 'em. Trust me fellas. Tomorrow night we're gonna get together. Come on now, we gotta have some type of fun around here, Tony?"

"Yeah, whatever man," he acquiesced.

"Marcus?"

"Fine, let's do it," he answered.

"Good, good. See y'all tomorrow… it's on."

CHAPTER 6

Jason had been out of prison five years now. He had his own place and a job working at a small town library that is actually the biggest he'd ever seen. He loved his job and was good at it. He wasn't just the head librarian and technician; he was the town's go-to man when it came to information. Jason knew where to find everything from the best prices on groceries to who was running in the local senate race. Thanks to a recent nonviolent felon program he was able to get his record cleared two years ago, so he no longer had that stigma to deal with. The best part about the library was it acted as the official library of the local group home so he got a lot of traffic from troubled teens, orphans, and young adults who had just it rough. It was a win-win situation. He was able to make a decent living and reach out to the troubled youth—something he set his mind on doing many years ago. He often looked back on his incarceration, just to keep himself grounded. He stayed in touch with Leon through letters, phone calls, and most recently, visits. It was through one of the old man's contacts that led him to this great job, and the apartment he was able to get almost immediately after his release. And he had a strong feeling that the guy who sold him his truck for dirt cheap was somehow connected to Leon too, though he couldn't prove it. The old man deftly avoided the questions when Jason asked.

"What's up Mr. J," the tall teen said as he walked through the double doors of the library with an armful of books.

"Hey Tony, you're back already? I know you didn't read all those that quick!" Jason said.

"Nah, only the top three; the other two aren't my speed—I skimmed through them though. What, you don't believe I could've taken all five of these down?" He held up the books as if saying "you're joking, right?"

Jason put his hands up and said "No sir, I know you very well could've." And indeed he did know. He first encountered this odd young man almost two years ago and almost immediately noticed how sharp and sophisticated he was. At the age of fourteen he was reading books that intimidated people twice his age, and the boy's vocabulary rivaled Jason's own, which was pretty extensive.

"What're you looking for? What's your speed?" he asked.

"Metaphysics and religion," Tony replied as he set the return books on the check-out counter.

Mr. J stared at him and waited for the punchline, and when one didn't come, he said "Wow." Tony looked confused. "You're the first fifteen-year-old I have ever heard say those two words, let alone want to read about them," Mr. J explained.

" I'm almost sixteen now." He shrugged, saying it like that explained it all.

"That you are," he said as he shook his head. "So is there anything specific within those genres you're interested in?"

"Well, that's the problem. I'm really not sure exactly what I"m looking for, or more correctly, where I should be looking. I'm just now starting my exploration on the subjects but I'm pretty sure one of those genres holds the key to some of the information I'm looking for," Tony finished thoughtfully.

"So is it God you're looking for, seeking out a religion so you can worship? Or are you approaching this from a purely academic standpoint?"

"All of that sounds good actually," the uncanny youth mused aloud, "are there any books on goddesses?"

Jason smiled and named off a long list of goddesses. As he did he noticed the eager gleam in the youth's eyes as he moved from behind the checkout desk.

"Follow me. I think you should start at the beginning and most would agree that it is ancient Kemet." Tony asked where that was. "Have you heard of the land of the Pharaohs?"

"Egypt," Tony answered.

"Yes sir. Many historians and scholars recognize that land as the hub of ancient civilization, and consequently the oldest gods and goddesses can be found there. There's an abundance of information on the culture, the religion and what life was like in those days. Here we go." He stopped and entered an aisle, with Tony close behind. "There's probably not a better selection on the subject anywhere in the state," Jason announced proudly. Much of the reason his library did have the widest selection on the topic was he got to put in new orders.

"As Tony began pursuing titles Mr. J named off some prominent authors: Cheik Anta Diop, Muata Ashby, Albert Churchward, Budge, Massey and Ellis…

"Take your time, and when you're ready come see me at the checkout." He left the young man to it and headed back to his desk. He found it very encouraging to see today's youth showing genuine interest in their history. And this kid here, he was something else… something special. Since Jason wasn't an actual staff member of Grover Homes he wasn't privy to this kid's history; he only knew what the teens chose to tell him. Tony told him that he lost his family in an accident and left it at that, but Jason didn't see any of the troubled signs that a lot of kids who have been through traumatic situations show. He might've been be a little reclusive, but there was a high level of resiliency about the boy.

"Hey Jason." Snapped out of his musing, he turned around to see his boss, Edward Fleming, coming up behind him. He greeted him and asked how things were going.

"Not too bad, but it looks like I'm going to need your expertise again." Edward was somewhere between fifty and seventy—it was hard to tell. A little shorter than Jason but almost frail-looking compared to him, but his posture was still excellent. He knew Jason's background, but he truly believed in second chances, and in time he came to value him. Edward Fleming was a good man with a heart of gold.

"Sure, anything you need just let me know and it's done," Jason said. They both paused as a pretty black girl approached them and asked Mr. J if he's seen Tony. "Yeah, he's somewhere in the ninth aisle." She politely thanked him and hurried off.

"Where was I… oh yes: the director at Grover Homes has gotten a request from the teachers at the school," Edward said. "They would like to have some kind of creative writing contest and publish the winner in the paper." He smiled as Jason's obvious interest flashed across his face. Jason rubbed his hands together and asked his boss where he fit in. "It seems you've made an impression on some of the teachers as well as most of the kids over there, because they asked for 'our' assistance. I know the meant you; I'm sure they said 'our' just to make me feel better."

Jason chuckled and said he'd love to help. "Do they have any specifics or do they want me to just come up with some ideas?"

"They have some suggestions, but they're pretty much giving you free reign over the project. You should be receiving an email shortly with all the information you'll need. I know you will come up with something good for them."

"Alright, this is going to be fun!" Jason said with sincere enthusiasm.

Tony sat cross-legged in the middle of an aisle, surrounded by books—a lot of books. After Mr. J led him to the row filled with books on his subject of interest, his eyes got big and shone with eager intensity. He wasn't daunted at all by the enormity of the task that lay before him...he was in his element. Now, as he sat there with five books in front of him and one open on his lap, scanning its index, his thoughts weren't fully on the present task. He was thinking about Javontay's match-making scheme and whatever plans he was cooking up—neither he or Marcus had a clue. They spoke about it after breakfast as they watched Tay smoothly approach Jamesha and then Ashley as the girls and boys left the main cottage. Tay had a way with girls so it was no surprise that both girls were smiling or giggling at some point during their talk. Ashley had even waved at Tony when Javontay walked away from her. Now he was nervously anticipating what was to come.

The only girl he had ever been close to was his best friend Kadence, but there was no denying that he felt some kind of way about Ashley. That is, when he actually looked at her without an assignment of some sort between them. He hadn't quite sorted through those feelings yet. Looking back on how he felt about Kadence at ten and eleven years old, he knew now that he loved her, but when he looked at Ashley something else stirred within him… he pushed those thoughts aside and focused on the task at hand. He'd think about all that later.

"Hi Tony," Ashley said, flashing her white teeth and small gap that Tony found alluring.

"Oh hey Ashley," he said clumsily as he fumbled with the book in his lap.

She asked him what he was reading as she entered the aisle gracefully and sat down across from him, a little to his right. Her lovely fragrance that reminded him of a mixture of fruit and flowers instantly filled the aisle. Her shirt hugged her torso, exposing just a bit of belly. He looked down at his book and cleared his throat.

"Um, I'm researching ancient goddesses. Mr. J said I should start with ancient Egypt because they have the oldest religion.

This whole row," he pointed, "and those too, are all books about ancient Egypt."

"Looks like you have your hands full," she said. "I'll leave you alone so you can concentrate if—"

"No, that's okay. You're not bothering me." He closed the book in his lap and put it on the stack beside him. "Even I can't read all these today, and you know I love to read," he said.

"You sure would try, though," she said, and smiled. He sheepishly agreed and smiled with her. They both looked at each other and locked eyes. Captivated by her beauty, he thought maybe now he should tell her just how beautiful she is.

"I like you Tony… Do you like me?" she asked shyly, speaking before he could.

"Yeah, I like you too. You're really beautiful." A weight seemed to lift from his shoulders as the words left his lips and he sat up straighter. "I didn't know you really liked me though," he went on, "I mean, I couldn't tell."

"That's because you were so focused on the schoolwork, but I definitely dropped you some hints. I just didn't want to seem too thirsty."

"So what did Tay say to you this morning?" Tony asked suspiciously.

"He told me that you like me." She grinned mischievously and he flushed with embarrassment. "I told him I already knew you did And I told him I like you too."

"Oh, you knew I did?" he asked playfully.

"A girl knows when a boy likes her. I don't know how; we just do." She winked at him and they both laughed.

"Leave it to Tay and his matchmaking," he said.

"Are you mad at him for telling me?"

"Nope, I'm happy at him for telling you," he said with intentional bad grammar. She giggled and then they both sat comfortably silent for a moment.

Ashley spoke first, letting him know that Tay also told her about his plan to meet up tonight. With raised eyebrows, she asked Tony what the exact plan was.

"I don't know; he didn't tell us. He just talked us into getting together. Knowing Tay, we'll probably be playing three-on-three basketball."

"I know Jamesha will have the full scoop as soon as I get back," Ashley said.

"Are you going to come with us if we get you?" he asked, as stoic as possible.

She stood up and modestly smoothed out her shirt while Tony stood up too and tried not to stare, smoothing out his own shirt that didn't have a wrinkle on it. There wasn't much room between them as they stood across from each other in the aisle. Tony could feel the heat coming from her body. She looked at him and smiled in a way that made her top lip curve up just a little more on the left side than the right.

"Of course I'm going to come with you," she said. And as if to reassure him she wasn't playing, she closed the gap between them and wrapped her arms around his neck. He instinctively, but a little clumsily, put his arms around her waist.

"I'm not playing basketball, though," she whispered up into his neck. His pulse quickened and he held her a little tighter, fearing he might fly away.

"Me neither—I'm no good at it," he responded in the crook of her neck, his lips lightly touching her skin as he spoke. She shivered and tightened her embrace too.

After what felt like minutes, they released their hold on each other. Ashley picked up the two books she brought with her and told him she would see him later.

He stood there speechless and watched her go, feeling like he was on a cloud. He knew he wouldn't be ignoring these feelings anytime soon.

"I see you went straight for the heavy stuff."

Tony's heart nearly jumped out of his chest as he spun around to face the voice that startled him. "Man, you can't be sneaking up on people like that!"

"My bad, Tony, I didn't mean to," Jason said with his arms up and palms out as he entered the aisle. "So did you find what you were looking for?" Jason asked around a smirk.

Tony quickly composed himself. "That's not funny, man; I could've had a heart attack or something."

"Nah, you're too young."

"Not true. I read about a fifteen-year-old basketball player dropping dead from sudden and inexplicable cardiac arrest," the teen said with exaggerated seriousness.

"Good thing you don't play basketball then, huh?" Jason retorted, and they both laughed.

After the laughter died down Mr. J asked him if he'd found anything yet. He said not exactly, but he knew he was in the right place. Tony picked up the six books that were on the floor, put one back on the shelf and said he would start with those five. Mr. J looked at the books in Tony's arms.

"Well, I see you're not playing around, huh? Those should keep you busy for a while," Mr. J said and then he gave him some advice, telling him not to just read but study, ruminate and cross-reference with other sources, and most importantly think for himself. The teen looked thoughtfully at the books he was holding and told Mr. J that it made sense.

"Did you see that girl you're always studying with yet? I told her you were back here."

"Uh… yeah, she just left before you got here—I saw her," he said awkwardly.

Mr. J just smiled. "Hey," he said, "I came back because I just received some info you might like to hear." He told him about the school at Grover Homes asking him to help them put a creative writing contest together. "First prize is fifty bucks, second place is thirty and third gets twenty." He paused and then added, "All three get their work published in the paper." That got Tony's full attention. He asked what the criteria were. Mr. J told him he would have the full details and instructions posted in the cottages this evening, before he went home.

"Are you picking the winners?" Tony asked.

"Not by myself, no; it will be me and two of the teachers. So are you in or what?"

"You know it," Tony said without missing a beat.

"Good. You have an excellent chance of getting published. Come on, let's check those books out."

Attention Residents of Grover Homes:

Grover Academy is holding a creative writing contest, hosted by your favorite librarian, and all are welcome. The topic is dreams. Everyone has dreams: the kind when you're sleeping or the kind you strive to reach while you're awake.

What do dreams mean to you? How do they affect what you do in life, if at all? Tell us in a written poem, a spoken word poem or prose, or write a short story.

1st place prize is $50.00

2nd place prize is $30.00

3rd place prize is $20.00

...All winners will be published in the paper!

The rules are simple: Absolutely no swearing, no plagiarism—all writings must be original, collaborations are permissible .

Put your dreams on paper and bring them to life. The deadline for submissions is one week from tomorrow.

Good luck. And remember, the library is always at your disposal.

-Mr. J

Tony finished reading the flier, read it again, then pulled a poem from his folder that he'd written months ago, and read it. He memorized the poem soon after penning it, but for some reason looking at it on paper made it more real. He immediately knew this was the poem he had to submit, although he briefly toyed with the idea of writing something new. He almost felt like it would be cheating by submitting an old piece. But, the energy that coursed through his entire being, the goosebumps that stood out on his arms and the fine hairs that were raised on the back of his neck when he recited this poem were too compelling to be ignored. This was the one. Feeling sure of his decision, Tony put his poem back in his folder and headed for his room. Javontay and Marcus were already back in the room and from the looks of it, something was up.

"What are you guys trippin' about now?" Tony asked as he came in and stood next to Marcus, who was clearly upset with Tay.

"Man, this fool told Teresa I like her!" Marcus said, outraged.

Tony was instantly brought back to his earlier encounter with Ashley. If it went half as good as that, he didn't see what the big deal was.

"How is that a bad thing? What happened?" Tony asked.

"The timing was all wrong, man. I told him I'd tell her when I was ready—"

"Hey, I was just trying to speed things up," Tay cut in defensively, "she told me she liked you too!"

"Marcus, what happened?" Tony asked more forcefully. Marcus shook his head, and then responded in a softer tone.

"I ate one of those burritos from the vending machine…" he paused, but was still shaking his head as if in total disgrace. "I had the bubble-guts and I was headed for the bathroom when Teresa saw me."

Javontay, his smirk gone, approached Marcus and put a hand on his shoulder consolingly. "Damn, Marcus, I told you about eating those machine burritos; they're always expired," he said solemnly.

"I know, I know but… they're so good," Marcus said, still shaking his head.

Forcing himself not to laugh, Tony repeated his question softer, with more patience. "What happened, Marcus? You have to tell us so we can prepare for damage control if we need to."

Marcus sighed. "It actually went pretty good at first," he started, "we laughed and she said she kind of knew that I liked her—something about 'girls always know.' She said she liked me too. Then my gut started doing backflips and I knew I had to get out of there, but I tried to control it because I wanted to keep talking to her, and I didn't want her to think I was trying to hurry up and get away from her." He blew out a breath and continued. "We did get to finish, but right as she started walking away I… I farted, man. And it wasn't quiet."

No one said anything for a long moment. Then Tony put his hand on Marcus's other shoulder and spoke. "It's not your fault; nobody can control the bubble-guts, man."

All three of them erupted in hysterical laughter until tears were coming from their eyes. When the laughter subsided, Marcus was the first to speak. "Do you think she's still feelin' me?"

"Yeah," Tony said optimistically.

"Listen," Tay said, "She definitely heard the fart, but I guarantee you she acted like she didn't, so you're good. Don't worry about it."

Marcus thought about that for a second and he brightened up a bit. "We're going to find out for sure tonight, right?" he said.

"Alright, tell us about this master plan you've hatched up," Tony said with some enthusiasm that both Marcus and Tay noticed, by the conspiratorial glance they gave each other.

"Check it out," Tay said, "Big Mike is working the night shift and you know he only does one round at about eleven. Once he does his round, we're out the window and going to meet the girls. They'll be waiting for us behind the main cottage. Our rendezvous point is the game room." Marcus and Tony looked a bit skeptical when they heard the game room. "Don't worry, we'll get in—I got this." Tay assured them.

"I got another one for you—" she whispered into the cell phone she wasn't supposed to have. "Yeah she's pretty! Alright, I'm sorry… Me and two other girls are sneaking out at about eleven tonight. We're meeting up with some boys from another cottage—" She smacked her lips in annoyance at the response from the person on the other end before continuing. "You have to get her after we meet up with them, though… Maybe an hour, maybe more… That's not my problem. I don't get paid for that… We'll be coming out of the back of the main cottage… I have to go… Alright!"

She pushed the end button and turned the power off. Her two roommates were still in the shower, but she didn't want to chance it. She took her shower early so she would be able to have the room alone long enough to make her call unnoticed. She didn't want to text either, because she couldn't pay attention to her surroundings at the same time. She let out an anxious breath. She felt bad lying to the girls, but she had a job to do and if she didn't do it, they would put her back on the streets, forced to sell herself just to make enough to eat. She would never go back to that. As long as she could get away with being a seventeen year old homeless girl, getting a free place to sleep and decent food, she was going to do it. At this rate she could be here at Grover Homes for another three years when she turned twenty. She laughed sardonically… she'd really be twenty-two and by then she should have enough money saved up. She knew her usefulness would run out by then and she would need it all to get a good start at living on her own.

But right now, thanks to her looks, she could easily pass for a seventeen-year-old girl; not to mention the phony paperwork and the few people who worked here that were on The Syndicate's payroll. She wasn't a cruel person, she didn't take pleasure in being perfidious, and honestly she genuinely liked some of the other girls. And the boy… she liked him a lot; he would never find out what she was doing—she would make sure of that. Yeah, she was older than him, but not by that much; they could still make it work. She really liked him and he definitely liked her, but she also knew he wouldn't if he ever learned what she was involved in. But she had to survive, and by any means necessary, she would.

❖   ❖   ❖

"Kiss me," Ashley said.

He leaned in and pressed his lips to hers. They were just soft and luscious as they looked. She gently parted her lips and slowly but methodically inserted her tongue; she found his and teased it, softly urging him to touch hers. He did and the sensation went through his whole body, making him feel warm and tingly like all of his senses were being massaged. He closed his eyes as if the pleasure was too much to bear feeling and seeing at the same time. He felt her soft hands caress the side of his face and run through his short, curly hair. His eyes opened and he pulled back.

The face now looking at him was not Ashley's, it was Kadence's.

"I love you, Tony," she said.

Her face changed again and it was Neith.

"Tony, I told you, you would never forget me and I will never leave you."

"Tony!" Marcus's rough whisper and even rougher shaking snapped him awake.

"Come on, it's party time," Tay said as he pulled a sweater over his head.

"Already, did Big Mike do his round?" Tony asked as he slid his shoes on and grabbed a light jacket.

"Yup, and I don't wanna leave the girls waiting too long. That wouldn't be very chiver… What's the word I'm looking for Tony?"

"Chivalrous," Tony said with a smirk.

"Yeah, that's it." He paused and looked at Tony. "How in the heck do you fall asleep so quickly? I've never seen anyone go into a dead sleep as fast as you." Tony shrugged and told him it's been like that since he can remember. "Alright y'all, fix your beds so it looks like someone's still in it, and let's go." Tay was already making his way to the window, while Marcus and Tony finished covering up their fake bodies. He suddenly stopped, turned back to face them and reached into his pocket. "Almost forgot," he said as he pulled out a pack of Trident gum and passed each of them a stick, "that would've been tragic." They gratefully accepted the gum and popped it in their mouths. As Tony cracked up Tay popped the piece into his mouth and smiled mischievously at Marcus.

"I'll go first," Tay said as he lifted up the window, and with the ease of a natural athlete, jumped out. Tony went next, and then came Marcus. None of them had any trouble landing from the short drop. They straightened themselves out and quickly surveyed their surroundings.

Grover Homes was really a manor an old rich guy donated to the state about fifteen years ago. The estate consisted of the main mansion which was the main cottage—the boys' current destination—and several garages and guest houses that now served as residences, the school, gym, and a maintenance building. Grover Homes was literally in a grove; trees were neatly surrounding the whole landscape, obscuring the group home from the main thoroughfare. There was a big yard in the front shaped like an oblong circle with a gravel road going all the way around it and veering off at different places, leading to the other buildings. The school cottage was off to the right, fifty or so yards, diagonally to the main cottage's front yard. In the back was a huge bare yard almost the size of an entire football field. At one end was the girls cottage and at the other end was the boys.

The three boys quickly made their way across the field, sticking to the shadows just beyond the glow of the powerful floodlights. They didn't talk at all; they were all consumed with their own thoughts of the fast-approaching tryst. Soon they came upon the back of the main cottage and Tay led them to an obscure-looking side door. The door seemed much older than the rest of the building but it looked like it belonged more than the recently restored façade did. He tapped the door lightly then waited. Within moments the door was opened and the boys crowded in. No one spoke until they entered the game room's lounge area where Ashley and Teresa were lounging on the couches.

"How did y'all get in here?" Marcus asked, sounding more than a little impressed.

"We have our ways," Jamesha answered as she followed them in. In true teenage awkwardness, the boys stayed with each other and so did the girls.

"I guess that means you're not going to tell us," he stated.

"A girl's gotta keep some secrets," she said teasingly. "Javontay, I want to show you something I found."

Breaking the teenage standoff, Jamesha walked over to him took his hand, and led him from the game room to one of the many niches, corridors, hallways, or rooms to be found in the mansion.

Marcus was nervous. He still wasn't fully past letting one loose in front of Teresa. Was she going to bring it up? Laugh at him? Embarrass him in front of everyone? She was smiling at him invitingly, but that could just be to get him to let his guard down. Tony seemed to sense his trepidation, so he broke the ice.

"Did you guys hear about the contest?" Tony asked as he approached the couch Ashley had chosen to sprawl on. His earlier meeting with her had given him a sense of courage he hadn't known before. Ashley was wearing faded blue jeans, white Reeboks and some type of white sleeveless blouse-shirt that showed off her beautifully toned chocolate skin. He sat down on the left arm of the couch, next to her legs. Marcus followed, sitting next to Teresa who was dressed in a hooded powder blue velour outfit; the hooded top was resting on the arm of the couch. She had a white shirt on with the word HOT spelled in rhinestones; the sleeves stopped just after her shoulders, exposing her honey-colored skin. A pair of white Nikes completed the outfit.

"What contest?" Marcus asked, more interested than he really was, but clearly glad for the icebreaker.

"You didn't hear about it either, Ashley?!" Tony asked, feigning shock at her lack of knowledge.

"What contest?" Marcus asked Teresa, "You know what he's talking about?"

"I have no clue," she said with a shrug.

"Tony, what are you talking about? There ain't no contest," Ashley said playfully, yet clearly intrigued.

"Oh yes there is, and since my greatest competition doesn't even know about it my chances of winning just got a lot better. Never mind, forget I ever said anything about it."

"Okay, okay tell us!" Ashley pleaded.

"Is it a French fry eating contest?" Marcus asked hopefully.

Teresa giggled. "You would lose if it was," she said and he looked at her with his eyebrows raised.

"Is that a challenge?" he asked smoothly.

"Whenever you're ready," she shot back just as smoothly.

"Be careful, that girl loves fries. My money is on Teresa," Ashley said seriously.

Relieved to have broken up the awkwardness between Marcus and the girl he obviously adored, Tony smiled. "Alright, I give up; I'll tell you. But you guys should really start reading the bulletin board in the cottages." He paused and gave everyone a stern parental stare. They all smacked their lips and rolled their eyes. "Mr. J and the teachers put together a creative writing contest," Tony said. Marcus exhaled, slapped his stomach, where he was now sitting next to Teresa on the couch.

"Looks like I'm gonna have to sit this one out," he said, "y'all know writing makes me hungry and I'm trying to watch my figure." Teresa giggled and rubbed his belly. "I like your figure, so I'm gonna pass too—so I can watch it with you," she said and they both laughed.

"We get to come up with whatever we want," Tony continued, "poems, short stories, prose... and the topic is dreams." He recited the rest of Mr. J's memo. Ashley listened intently as she subtly sat up and pulled him down from the arm of the couch to sit comfortably next to her. Marcus and Teresa were no longer paying them any attention as they were fully engrossed in their own conversation.

"I know you're going to submit something? You've got to. I've read some of your stuff and it's definitely good enough to be published," Tony said to Ahsley while he studied her face.

"I don't know," she said hesitantly, "you know I really don't like to share my writings."

"You share 'em with me. And besides, you don't have to submit an old piece; you could do something new—something you're not that attached to."

"I share my work with you because I trust you and… I really like you. And even if I do write something new it would still be personal to me. I don't know; I just feel like I expose myself every time I write."

"See, that's what makes you so good, you don't hold back so it's always real and relatable. Maybe you should let other people get a glimpse of that."

"I'll think about it," she said after a thoughtful pause.

They went on talking and laughing, learning about each other in ways they hadn't before, becoming more than study partners. Marcus and Teresa were also learning about each other on deeper levels, finding common interests and bonding. Javontay and Jamesha returned with snacks and drinks from the kitchen— Much to Marcus's and Teresa's delight—and soon they were all joking, laughing, and genuinely enjoying each other's company. In that moment, they all forgot that they were orphans living in a group home with no real family and nothing much to call their own. The level they got to know each other on was deep, yet simple: they got to be themselves, normal teenagers without their defensive guards up for the night. They shared some of their goals and hopes for the future and some of their past, each of them creating an affinity with the other that only comes through knowing that they have all been through a lot and experienced pain and loneliness of the same magnitude. They all became true friends.

"What time is it?" Ashley asked sleepily from where she rested in Tony's arms on the couch. Tony blinked his eyes open, noticed how quiet it was and saw the other two couples in similar states of half-consciousness. He smiled inwardly. He wouldn't mind having Ashley in his arms forever.

"It's 3:36," Tony said as he read the clock on the wall across from the couch he and Ashley were on.

"Man, school went by quick today," Marcus said through a yawn, "I don't even remember what we had for lunch," he mumbled. Teresa laughed where she lay on his belly. "It's 3:36 in the morning, goofy," she said. "Oh good, that means we didn't miss lunch," he shot back.

"We should be heading back," Jamesha said as she got up from where she and Tay were entwined, "we can always do this again."

"Not if we get caught," Tay said. Everyone, hearing the wisdom in those words, got up and started preparing to leave.

"Let's put everything back the way it was too, and throw the empty wrappers away," Tony said. They all did their part and left the game room the way they found it, then they made their way back to the door they came in through.

In the dark foyer each pair snuggled up against each other, preparing for their departure. Someone cracked the door open so a sliver of light pierced the darkness.

"We should walk you girls back," Tony said.

"Yeah, it's real dark out there," Marcus agreed.

"We'll be okay. There are three of us and it's no darker than it was when we first came out," Jamesha yawned.

"If there are more of us together it'll be easier for someone to see us too," Teresa said, "and I don't wanna mess this up." She squeezed Marcus tighter as she said it. The three boys reluctantly agreed as they hugged and kissed their girls goodbye. They exited first so the girls could lock up—they still wanted to keep their trump card a secret. Javontay, Marcus, and Tony quickly made the trek back to their cottage and into their room.

"Man, we should've let them walk us back," Ashley said as she looked into the darkness that surrounded them as they walked.

"It looks like the trees are moving towards us," Teresa said. Jamesha just kept walking, seemingly unaffected by their paranoia although she did glance around a couple of times.

"Let's just hurry up," Ashley said and quickened her pace.

They made it back to their cottage and quickly got to their window. Ashley opened it and started to climb in when she felt someone pull on her arm, halting her. "Wait till we get in, it's cold—" she stopped mid sentence as she turned around and saw Teresa held tight against a man dressed in black. One hand covered her mouth; the other held a knife pressed against Teresa's neck. The guy didn't appear to have a mask on, but the shadows hid every feature of his face except his cold eyes that twinkled from the moonlight, promising death as sure as the knife he held.

"If you scream I'll kill her. Now get inside and close the window," the man said in a calm businesslike manner that told the girls that this was not a game.

"Please let her go. I have some money inside; you can take it all. Just please let her go," Jamesha pleaded frantically as the man started backing away with Teresa. His eyes flickered to the window behind her and he hesitated, then she felt Ashley tug at her arm. Come on Jamesha, we can't help her like this. We can scream for help when we get inside and—"

Something snapped inside of Jamesha. She thought about the time they just spent together and the two years her and Teresa had known each other; the sisterly bond they formed. She couldn't lose someone else she loved, someone who didn't judge her and saw her as family. She had to do something. She screamed angrily and launched forward. "Let her go!"

The big kidnapper was caught off guard by the brazen move, but he quickly recovered. With one swift motion he took the blade from Teresa's neck and shoved her at the oncoming Jamesha. The girls collided and knocked Ashley down in the process. The man bolted into the shadows of the trees and was long gone before the girls untangled themselves.

"Come on, hurry up. We gotta get inside!" Ashley said as she helped both of the girls stand up. They made it in safely and silently slid the window shut behind them, just in time.

"Is everything alright in here?" Nicole, the night staff, asked as she shined the beam of her flashlight on each of the girls' beds that they were now in. "I thought I heard a scream."

"It wasn't us, we're fine. We were just talking," Jasmesha said.

"Well hold it down; everybody else is sleeping—like you girls should be," Nicole scolded.

"Sorry. Goodnight Miss Johnson," Ashley said. Nicole Johnson shook her head and closed their door. The girls breathed a sigh of relief and immediately jumped out of their beds. Teresa didn't move though; she laid there with a sickened expression on her face, clutching the covers in her small fists. Jamesha and Ashley went to her bed and sat down.

"You're okay now Teresa," Jamesha said while she wiped away the tears coming down the pretty girl's face. Ashley pulled her tangled hair away from her cheek and noticed a bruise that must have come from her collision with Jamesha.

"I thought he was going to take me somewhere and… rape me," Teresa sobbed.

"I wasn't going to let him take you, girl," Jamesha said fiercely. She pulled Teresa into an embrace and they squeezed each other. Ashley put her arms around both girls and huddled with them.

Moments later, Teresa calmed down and attempted to straighten herself up, but she was still obviously shaken up; her body was trembling as she moved. "Girl, you went crazy… he wasn't ready for that," she said as she looked right at Jamesha.

"Yeah, what were you thinking?! He could've killed her," Ashley said somberly.

"I wasn't thinking, but I knew I couldn't just let him take her. Besides, he wasn't here to kill anybody—he was gonna rape her. Trust me." Jamesha knew all too well about the horrors of sexual abuse. She ran away from home to escape it and found herself, young and vulnerable, exposed to the streets and all the horror it had to offer a damaged black girl. She was victimized but she was no victim; she was a survivor.

"Thank you, Mesha. I'd rather die than go through that… again. I mean that," Teresa said. They all fell silent as the weight of her words hit them, causing each of them to relive their own experience and realize they felt the same way.

"You think we should tell the staff about this, even though we know they won't believe us?" Teresa asked, breaking the silence.

"They definitely won't believe us. They'll just flip it on us and punish us for being outside at night," Ashley agreed.

"Maybe that's what's been happening to the other girls," Jamesha mused aloud.

"Everybody knows those girls ran away. Girls and boys run from here all the time. I've thought about running away a couple of times," Ashley said.

"Some do," Jamesha said, "but I knew some of those girls and I'm not so sure that's what really happened anymore. And even if they did run away, how do we know that guy or a guy like him didn't get them before they made it? You're right though, it won't do us any good to tell the staff—unless we got the dude hogtied and stuffed under the bed. They don't care."

"Come on, let's get some sleep," Ashley said, not noticing the sideways look Jamesha cast her way.

The next day each of the girls related what happened to them during their walk back to their cottage. Teresa was still pretty shaken up and she nearly broke down when she told Marcus in a quiet hallway at school. Marcus comforted her as best as he could, but he couldn't hide his anger. He understood why they didn't report it to the staff, but something had to be done. Javontay and Tony were stunned. Tay couldn't find any words, but Tony, almost immediately, fired off a bunch of questions at Ashley. Did they notice the guy's skin color? Did anything stand out besides the guy being a predator? Did they see a car? Ashley answered no to all of them.

"Well, if we do get together again, we're coming to get you guys at your cottage and we're walking you back. I don't care about Jamesha's secret way in—we won't look." He blew out an angry breath. "I knew we shouldn't have let you guys walk back by yourselves," he finished, clearly upset with himself for not being more persistent about walking them back.

Ashley affectionately studied Tony's face as they sat next to each other in one of the aisles in the library, one of his usual spots. The library was big enough that if Mr. J didn't know exactly where he was, somebody looking for him could spend ten minutes trying to find him.

"If...? I was going to suggest we get together again next weekend. Really, it wasn't that bad; I mean nobody got hurt. And it wasn't you guys' fault," Ashley said.

Tony frowned, somewhat taken aback by her dismissal of the near kidnapping of her roommate.

"You boys aren't the only ones who have been through rough and dangerous situations out there. Some of us have been through much worse than what that guy did. We're a lot tougher than you know," she said with a confident smile.

"I saw Teresa," he said, "and she definitely looks spooked. I think it may have affected her more than you think. And just because you have been through bad things before, it doesn't extenuate—lessen the severity of—" he clarified, "the other bad things that may happen."

"Yeah, you're right," she said and put a hand on his knee.

"Did you ask the other girls if they saw anything recognizable about the guy?" he asked, not quite ready to let it go.

"No, but it was dark so I'm sure we all saw the same thing," Ashley said.

"Everyone perceives reality differently." Ashley cocked an eyebrow at his mystical statement and he shrugged. "I read it in a book and it stuck with me because I've seen how true it is." He paused pensively. And much to Ashley's relief, he changed the topic to something lighter. "I know it hasn't been long since I asked you and there's a lot going on, but have you thought any more about submitting something for the contest? No pressure," he said timidly, and they both smiled, "but I'm a firm believer that when you have something good to say, you should say it."

She actually hadn't thought about it at all since last night; she was too busy enjoying just talking and being next to him. But she knew he wasn't just gassing her up about liking her writings, so if nothing else, she knew she'd participate just for him. "Yeah, I think I will submit something," she said with a big smile. He returned the smile and said good. Ashley asked him if he had already started writing something for the contest yet and he told her he already had something ready.

"Of course you would already be ahead of everyone," she said. And he explained the subject was one he'd already written about before.

"Do you want to hear it? I have it memorized," he asked enthusiastically. She said she would love to.

He grabbed her hands and they stood up together; he backed up a few steps and then began. As he recited his poem he became animated, moving his hands in harmony with the inflectional changes in his voice. His eyes flared up with a passion that captivated Ashley. There was strength that radiated from him as he spoke and he gave off the impression that he was watching the poem come to life right before his eyes. His fervor was infectious and it drew her in like a blazing beacon guiding her imagination. When Tony was finished, Ashley's eyes stayed closed as if she was still lingering in the world of his poem. After a moment, she slowly opened her eyes.

"Wow!" she breathed, "That was intense." He asked her if she understood it all. "There are a few words you'll have to break down to me later, but overall, yes, I understood it very well. It had more to do with your delivery than anything else. I'm never gonna be able to see my dreams the same way again." He asked her if she thought it was good enough to submit and she said it was perfect, especially if he recites it the way he just did for her. She clutched his arm with excitement and told him she really thought he was going to win. He smiled and blushed a little at the confidence she placed in him.

"There's some good competition out there. Have you heard Lyle or David's spoken word poetry before? They're really good too."

"Nope, I haven't, but my money is still on you," she said.

"Glad you have my back," he said.

"Always," she responded as she slipped into his arms and laid her head against his chest. He wrapped his arms around her and they held each other.

"Well, I better get back with the rest of the class before Miss Weburg notices she's missing one," Ashley said as she reluctantly let go of Tony.

"See you later," he said.

"Later."

Tony watched her leave, then sat back down and started reading again. He didn't get too far because Mr. J entered the aisle and sat down with him. Tony was kind of glad he showed up because something had been nagging at him.

"Hey, I was just thinking about something: Did you purposely make it so the contest would fall on my birthday?"

"How could I? I don't know what day it is; I knew it was in May but that's it. Plus, I didn't decide the actual day of the contest; the teachers did," Mr. J replied innocently. Tony said he'd take it as a good sign then. Or a bad one, he thought to himself... This was the time of year that reminded him of the tragedy he suffered what seemed like a lifetime ago now. He pushed that thought aside, though, and asked his real question.

"Do you know of a goddess called Neith?"

"Yeah, she's an ancient Egyptian goddess of creation and war. She is recognized as the oldest goddess; her worship goes all the way back to pre-dynastic times—before 3,200 B.C.E. Neith is known by many names and has many attributes." He paused and asked if Tony found her in one of the books.

"Uh... maybe," he equivocated, "I was just wondering if there was more you could tell me about her." He was almost trembling with barely-contained excitement.

"Sure. Like I was saying, she has many names and attributes; just keep in mind that they aren't separate entities, they are different elements and extensions of the one God, who is in the form of the Goddess." Mr. J paused to make sure he got that before he continued. "Neith is androgynous, meaning as the creator she encompasses both genders, and at the same tme, transcends them. In her warrior aspect she's a protector, hence her symbols: the bow, arrows, and shield. In one of her creator aspects she's known by the name Mehenit and is said to have woven creation into existence, thus her other symbol, the knitting spool—"

"Wait a minute, what?!" Tony almost yelled.

Jason stopped and looked at the boy questioningly. Tony asked him where the book that had that information in it was. Without waiting for an answer, he stood up and headed for the ancient Egyptian aisle. He stopped abruptly, realizing he left Mr. J behind and he was probably looking a little crazy. He took a deep breath and composed himself. When Mr. J caught up with him he put a hand on Tony's shoulder and asked him if he was alright.

"Yeah, yeah just a little excited to have found what I've been looking for, sorry," Tony said slowly.

"That's alright, I know the feeling; trust me. Come on." He motioned the boy forward. When they made it to the right aisle Jason scanned a few shelves and then pulled a small, thin book from one of them. "You probably never even noticed this one," he said, "over the years of studying I've come to realize that a lot of the smaller books have the most profound insights. It's mostly because they stay away from using all those flowery words." He flipped the book open, found the right page and handed it to Tony. The boy took the book, read a few lines and sucked in a sharp breath.

The drawings were crude, compared to his dream, but there was no mistaking it; this was the Goddess who visited him on the night of his accident. And the descriptions of her, the symbol of the knitting spool… yes, this is Neith! He sat down, almost overwhelmed with emotion. There were only three pages describing her, but it was enough. He flipped through those three pages at least four times within minutes, paying particularly close attention to one paragraph" *Net (Neith) is also called Mehenit, the Goddess of weaving. She wove her own clothing, which is the material universe and all that abides therein. The aspiration of the Kemetic follower is to undress her and behold her real, abiding form and therefore the underlying essence of all that exists.*"

"I know the limit is five, but do you think—"

"Go ahead. I know you'll take care of it like it's your own," Mr. J said.

Tony closed the book, set it in his lap and then rested his head against the back of the bookshelf he was sitting against. Calmness settled over him but the bitterness swarmed him like a cloud of gnats. Neith is real… God is real. So why didn't she save his family? He didn't get it. She's a protector, but she didn't protect Lisa or Tommy.

"Can I ask you something Tony?" Mr. J said and sat down, rescuing Tony from his heart aching thoughts. Still looking up with his eyes closed, Tony said yeah. "Why are you always in the library? I know you love to read, but I sense there's more to it than that. Is the group home that bad?"

Tony sat quietly, deep in thought, and then gave Jason a measured look. Apparently satisfied with what he saw, Tony opened up.

"No, Grover isn't that bad, really, but there are no real activities or interaction between us and the staff. As long as we follow the rules they don't seem to notice us. I mean, the writing contest is the most exciting thing we've had since I've been here. Why the library, though?" He waved his arms out wide. "Because here, I can escape my reality and learn about it at the same time. When I read Orson Scott Card, I become Ender; when I read Simon R. Green, I become Owen Dealthstalker and when I read R.A. Salvatore I become Drizzt Do'urden." He held up the book of the Goddesses. "And when I study literature on past human thought and culture, I feel like I'm connecting with my ancestors and learning about myself, and it inspires me." As Tony paused,

Jason looked at him with wonder, impressed by the young man's insight and wanting to hear more.

"You know, when I was seven years old I started reading out loud for my little sister and older brother at bed time. They loved it! We all got caught up in the stories; it got to the point where we looked forward to being told it was bedtime! That was our night at the movies, and the best times of my life. I surround myself with books because that's the only way I can see Lisa and Tommy again. With every book, every story I read, I feel like I have them with me, enjoying the adventure, laughing with me… living."

He stopped as he heard the slow patters of tears landing on the cover of the book resting on his lap. He wiped his face with the palm of his hand and rubbed the book against his shirt. He told Jason the story of how his brother and sister died and then how he ended up in Grover Homes after losing his mom too. Tony cried tears that shook his whole body, tears that had been aching to be released for years. He always held it in, never letting his emotions show because he felt that once he did he would end up getting close to someone, only to lose them. But he always yearned to tell someone how much he missed his family, to find a release for the pain that filled his heart like the words in a horror novel with a sequel.

When Tony was finished, Mr. J shared his story. He told him that he could relate with a lot of the kid's childhood and that's why he still worked at the library, though other job opportunities came his way. He opened up about his stint in prison and even told Tony about his best friend, Leon. Intellectually, they formed a bond a long time ago, but during these forty or so minutes of talking, they became true friends.

CHAPTER 7

"Damn! I can't believe they got psycho-kidnappers running around here… this is nuts!" Javontay exclaimed from his top bunk.

"He's lucky I wasn't there; it really would've got nuts," Marcus said calmly. He was so distraught he didn't even finish his entire plate at dinner.

"We have to at least try to do something. Who knows how long this has been happening," Tony said.

"The staff sure don't give a damn. You've been here long enough to hear the stories about girls running away, Tony, but even the other girls don't believe most of them really ran," Marcus said.

"What could we do anyway?" Tay asked. "We don't even know who this guy is or even what he looks like."

They all thought about it for a while and then the beginnings of an idea formulated in Tony's head. "We could set him up; ambush him. You know?" He got excited as he went on. "We'll use the girls as bait… no, we'll use one of the girls as bait and then all three of us will be hiding, waiting for him to come out. As soon as he does, we'll jump his ass!"

"Yeah, I like that!" Marcus said, just as excited.

"Ashley said she wants us to get together next weekend, so we can do it then," Tony said.

"Okay, that sounds good and all, but whose girl is gonna be the bait?" Tay said.

No one said anything as Tay's rational question sucked the enthusiasm out of the room. None of them wanted to put their girl in harm's way.

"Listen Tony," Tay said, breaking the silence, "don't take this the wrong way, but I don't think it should be Ashley."

"What do you mean by that?" Tony asked.

"Jamesha told me that Ashley was acting funny when that dude tried to take Teresa; like she didn't even try to help when Mesha ran at him—"

"Maybe she was too scared," Tony said defensively, although he definitely didn't sense any fear when he and her talked.

"That's not all though," Javontay went on, "she also told me when they got inside and started talking about the other girls that this might've happened to, Ashley defended the staff's claims that all the girls were just runaways. She even told Jamesha she shouldn't have run at the dude. I don't know. I'm just telling you how Mesha feels…"

"Are you saying Ashley has something to do with this?!" Tony said angrily.

"Hold on, Tony," Marcus jumped in, "he's not saying that; he's just telling you what Jamesha told him. Don't jump to any conclusions—none of us has a clue what's going on."

"My bad; you're right." Tony sighed.

"You know…" Marcus mused aloud, "there's something that just doesn't make sense to me." The other two remained quiet and waited for him to finish. "Think about it: did one of you guys tell anybody that we were going to meet up with the girls?" Tony and Tay both said no. "That means either the girls told someone or they let someone see them and someone else told," Marcus continued. "We hung out for a long time; how would anyone know how long we were going to be in there?"

"And if he was just lurking, why didn't he try to take one of them before they made it to the main cottage or even while they were on their way there?" Tony finished.

"I don't like this; I don't like this at all," Javontay said gravely.

None of them liked it, least of all Tony. He got a sick feeling in his stomach as he replayed the conversation he had with Ashley; she was just too indifferent or unfazed by it all. There was a way to find out what was going on with her though, or at least eliminate her from suspicion.

"It has to be Jamesha," Tony said.

"What?" Tay said.

"She has to be the bait. For one, she tried to fight so that eliminates her from being involved and it definitely shows that she's not too scared to carry out whatever plan we come up with. We can't put Teresa in that position again, and Ashley... well, we can use this to cross her off the list of suspicion."

"He's right, Tay," Marcus agreed.

"Yeah, I know," Tay said dejectedly. "I'll talk to her."

Kadence hadn't seen Tony since the funeral of his sister and brother, but she'd never stopped thinking about him. When he stopped showing up at school she asked her dad if he knew anything about what happened to him. He told her about his mom dying and him being placed in the system. "It's sad he has to go through all of this at his age," is how he ended the story. Afterwards, Kadence went to her room and cried. She felt so bad that he had to endure such pain and loss; it wasn't fair. She also felt guilty because besides the incident with her father's stroke, she never experienced any real adversity; she knew being denied sleepovers with friends and not being able to get certain outfits didn't count. And she knew she would break if she went through what Tony went through.

Kadence was familiar with the less fortunate kids though, so she understood very early that she was blessed. She had both of her parents in the same house and they were loving parents, not too strict but definitely disciplined. She had good grades and she was liked by most of the people she made contact with. As she got older she became a leader and someone who others looked to for advice. She was exceptionally goal-oriented so the boys and other teenage distractions never got in her way. She was classified as a square, but she didn't care. Kadence had a lot going for her; a good upbringing and hard work helped get her far. But she also had a gift that she never told anyone about.

She noticed it after the last dream she had, when her father recovered from his stroke. She felt that somehow Tony had something to do with it; she just couldn't figure out how. But she was determined to find the answer. When Kadence slept she always dreamed, but ever since Tony's presence in her dream she rarely had dreams about herself. Whenever she thought too hard about someone else throughout the day, for whatever reason, she was able to *see* their dream. She knew they weren't her own because she felt totally disconnected from them; there were no familiar feelings, no memories of her own and the people were vague. She didn't catch on until the night after she felt Tony's presence in her first dream. That night Kadence saw her mom's dream. Her mom was dreaming of a time before Kadence was born, a time when her parents were young. She felt a kind of love that she had never felt before and had thoughts that were foreign but oddly familiar because she heard bits and pieces of them expressed by her mom before. The connection was so profound that she saw exactly what day it was, what both her parents were wearing and even the weather outside.

The next morning, in the hospital room with her father, Kadence's mom began reminiscing and she recounted the memory she had dreamt about the night before.

"Your dad and I were so in love when we were young," she began in a far-off voice, as she gazed at her husband lying unconscious in the hospital bed. "All we wanted to do is be around each other. We skipped school one day just to walk around Lake Humble; we talked and laughed for hours that day. Your grandmother tore my butt up when she found out. Mr. Robinson saw us in the drugstore, though, and that's how we got caught." She finished with a shake of her head.

"It started raining, that's why you guys went in there, huh." Kadence tried to make it sound like a question but it came out like a stated fact.

"How did you know that? I never told anyone about that day." "Dad told me," she lied.

She tried it again, the next day, on a different person and the same thing happened: she saw the other person's thoughts, felt their emotions, and recalled the memories they experienced in their dream. She tried finding Tony's dreams to see if she could find some answers and maybe even communicate with him, but she got nowhere. She thought about him until she cried, but it was as if he didn't dream. She once read in a book that everybody dreams, but no matter how hard she concentrated on Tony she could not find his dreams. She didn't want to think about what that could mean, so she ignored the thought every time it surfaced in her head. In the process of searching for Tony, she honed her gift and began using it to help other people… and herself when she needed an advantage.

Five years ago she had dreams of becoming a youth counselor and it seemed more and more likely that she would not only become a youth counselor but a very good one. She joined the Youth Tutor Program (Y.T.P.), which gave her the opportunity to get great training and experience. Through the program she had been able to make a difference in the lives of kids that deal with some tough issues. She would tap into their dreams and help them deal with issues they suppressed or avoided and they grew to respect and, more importantly, trust her.

She started searching the internet for information that might help her learn more about her ability and maybe find others like herself. She learned some interesting things and met more than a few people who claimed to have extraordinary powers, but somehow those powers couldn't be used until they received a $49.95 donation from her. Kadence didn't get discouraged, though; she kept on sifting through the nonsense, hoping to find something useful.

Roselynn Mackey, the head guidance counselor of the Y.T.P. recently informed her of a four-day program that involved meeting with teenage girls at a group home and introducing a critical thinking group. She would get college credits for it too. Kadence didn't hesitate; she signed up immediately.

Now, she and three other girls she worked with were on their way to a hotel that was close to the group home. After the sixty-five minute drive they pulled into the Bayport Inn's parking lot and unloaded their belongings. Their rooms were already reserved. When they got into the lobby, Kadence called her dad to let him know she made it. Roselynn checked them in and got their room keys; she told them to get comfortable and then meet in her room for a briefing on what to expect for the next few days. Kadence and Marissa shared one room, Tasha and Jessica shared another.

"It's twelve-fifty six now. In about an hour or so we'll be heading over to the group home." Roselynn began in the formal tone she always used whenever she gave instructions. She stressed professionalism to the girls when it came to doing their job, but she also cautioned against being uptight and rigid when doing the actual counseling because, as she put it, "the objective is to create an environment in which those we are trying to help take us seriously, but feel comfortable enough to tell us what they need help with." So the four girls sat on the hotel's queen-sized bed with notepads, listening attentively as Roselynn spoke.

"Our work headquarters will be at the library," she continued, "I'm sure you are all aware that this county has the biggest library in the state, with the most comprehensive book selection." The girls beamed at the prospect of exploring the library. "So this excursion of ours has a dual purpose, the same purpose counseling itself has: teaching and being taught. Arrangements have been made for us to have full access to the library; our chaperone will be Jason Madison, the head librarian." The girls jotted the name down as Roselynn paused. "Remember that these are not your ordinary teenage girls. Most of them have been through traumatic situations and have been forced to grow up faster; some may have hardened themselves to hide their vulnerability. Your advantage is you're in the same age group as these girls. But you will lose that advantage if you come off as uptight or as a know-it-all. When you're interacting with these young women, remember that you know absolutely nothing about them or what they've been through. So your immediate objective is to find out by listening, asking questions, and never assuming."

Roselynn went over a few more things and answered questions some of the girls asked. As the girls were heading out to their own rooms Roselynn stopped them. "One more thing: there will be boys at the library who are also residents of the group home. Please be on your best behavior." With those final words and a few giggles, the girls finally left for their rooms.

Half an hour later Kadence was in her room by herself, while the other three girls were in the other room still talking about the "bad boys' ' they were hoping to see, and preparing themselves with makeup. Tasha, Jessica, and Marissa were a little boy-crazy but they usually kept their priorities in order. That didn't mean they wouldn't try to look extra cute. Kadence, on the other hand, was focused on the girls she was going to meet and what a great opportunity this was. She wished she could've met the girls in advance so she could use her gift, but she'd just have to rely on her natural intuition and people skills, which were just as effective at times.

Twenty-five minutes later they were pulling into a lot that seemed too small in contrast to the big Victorian-style library building. The group home mansion and its front yard were partially visible through the trees; Kadence noticed the nice pathway that connected it to the library. For a brief moment she wondered how close she came to being one of the girls she was here to counsel, walking that path to go home…

"Alright, here we are ladies," Roselynn said as she parked the van, "We're going to have about an hour before our first group, so we'll do introductions with Mr. Madison, let him show us around and then you can check the library out on your own. Are you girls ready?"

They smiled at each other and nodded. Kadence could tell the other girls were a little nervous, but she was calm as ever.

"Let's go show these girls someone cares about them," she said calmly as she got out of the van. The others followed, infused with confidence by Kadence's words.

CHAPTER 8

Nikki was excited. She knew she was going to win this contest; she was one of the best writers in the place. She knew it and so did everyone else. That's all she did was write, and she took it very seriously—a little too serious depending on who you asked. She walked around with a notebook and a pad of Post Its because she preferred writing notes to people over actually talking to them. She thought of television and video games as counterproductive, worse than being idle. If it wasn't educational she wanted nothing to do with it. They called her a nerd and she gladly embraced the title, even from her boyfriend, David. She wasn't totally square, though—her sneaking out to smoke a cigarette every night was a testament to that—but she had a goal she couldn't be sidetracked from.

She'd be eighteen in two months and she had to be able to support herself; she was determined to make it as a writer. She wanted to go to college and eventually, Nikki wanted to get custody of her six-year-old brother who was in a foster home. That's why she had to win this contest too, his birthday was coming up and she wanted to have a present for him at their next visit. She took a long pull on the Newport she was smoking and looked at its tiny coal. She'd have to kick this habit too; smoking was way too expensive.

She took her last drag, savoring the menthol taste that was so addicting, and then crushed the end against the side of the building and put it in her pocket. She would flush it later. She didn't like to litter and she definitely didn't want to leave any evidence. She put one foot on the green lawn chair, to climb back through her cottage window. The other foot didn't make it, though.

A gloved hand clamped over her mouth while an arm like corded steel snaked around her waist and she was easily lifted in the air and carried off. She tried to struggle, but her five-foot-one inch, hundred and sixteen pound frame wasn't up to the task. The most she managed to do was lose her glasses, the only expensive thing she owned. She was shoved in a car and a hood was placed over her head and she felt her hands and then her feet being bound together. All she could think about was her baby brother Jonathan, stuck in a foster home without her…

Mr. J, you have to help us. The staff don't care. We told them they weren't running away but they don't take us seriously," Jamesha rambled off frantically.

"Slow down. What's going on?" Mr. J said soothingly. "Start from the beginning."

"Nikki is gone… we were just talking the other day!" Jamesha was pacing back and forth in front of the checkout counter. Mr. J walked from behind his desk and led the girl to one of the tables.

"Alright, tell me what happened."

"Nikki and I were talking two days ago; she was all excited about the writing contest—you know she's *really* into that kind of stuff. Then this morning everyone's saying something happened to her and when I asked, they said the staff said she ran away last night. Nikki wouldn't run away though!"

"How do you know she wouldn't?" But as he asked the question, he knew Jamesha was right. He was familiar with Nikki and she was a very bright young lady who probably would've won the upcoming contest.

"Because she has nowhere to go!" Jamesha said with complete sureness. "Mr. J, girls talk and some of us are really close. Nikki did not run away from here. If she was going to go, she would've at least waited for the outcome of the contest—everybody knew she was going to win second place at least."

"Yeah, that is odd," he said. "So what do you think happened to her?"

"Somebody… took her." She paused and bit her bottom lip, debating whether to confide in him or not. "The other night me and some other girls—I'm not saying who 'cause I can't rat my girls out—we snuck out. We never left the grounds, though," she quickly added. "When we were coming back in a man came out of nowhere and tried to take Te— one of us, but we fought him and he ran off."

"Did you tell the staff?" At her sideways glance he held his hand up. "Okay, I get why you think you shouldn't have." Jason sat quietly for a moment and contemplated his next move. "There's not much I can do; I'm not a staff member at Grover. But I will find out what I can and voice my concerns to the people who can do something. Okay?"

"Okay. Thank you Mr. J." They both got up from the table, but before Jamesha walked away she spoke again. Mr. J, I've been in Grover Homes for three years and a lot of girls have gone missing since then. Most of them didn't run away; I know it." She looked at him gravely, searching his eyes for help, and then left the library and headed back to her cottage.

"Mr. Madison, we appreciate your concern, but we are very capable of handling these kinds of situations ourselves," Kent Foster, the director of Grover Homes, began. "We have alerted the authorities of the runaway and now it is up to them to do their job." He paused, clasped his hands in front of him on his desk, and looked at Jason earnestly. "I've been doing this job for thirteen years, the entire times Grover Homes has been open, and we have had many runaways. Some are found and returned, others move on. In each and every case we do all we can and we certainly follow proper procedure."

"With all due respect, I am not trying to tell you how to do your job, nor am I questioning your competence. It's just that a lot of these kids don't believe this particular girl ran away and neither do I, so I would be remiss if I didn't voice my concern." Jason made sure he put heavy emphasis on kids and girl. He noticed how Kent Foster seemed to avoid identifying her as anything other than a runaway and that bugged him on many levels. "Some of the kids believe Nikki and others were abducted. I'm just asking that you pass that information on to the authorities," Jason finished politely.

"Of course I will. And again, thank you for your concern; it's very admirable." Kent Foster stood up from behind his desk and walked to his window that held a beautiful view of the library. "You've got a really good job over there, Mr. Madison, and it seems you've made quite an impression on the residents and some of my teachers." He paused and turned to face Jason. "You must really value your position and take it serious."

Jason Madison came from the streets. He'd dealt with gangbangers, drug dealers, and all kinds of shysters; going to prison exposed him to the more insidious dangers as well. He saw malicious prison guards and systemic racism. So he knew to watch out for the subtle dangers, and right now his senses just tingled a little. Did the director just threaten his job? Or was this a mind-your-own-business warning?

"Of course I do; I love my job and serious is the only way to take it," Jason replied as he looked the director squarely in the eyes.

"I agree. And I'm glad Edward hired you."

"I guess I'll get back to it then," Jason said as he stood up and then left Kent Foster's office without waiting for a reply. Kent Foster smiled, walked to his desk, and picked up the phone.

The guy was no doubt power tripping, but was he being intentionally negligent? Is there something sinister going on? Jason didn't get that feeling. Kent Foster did report Nikki Olson as a runaway; he showed Jason the paperwork, so technically he did do his job. But he sure wasn't going to go above and beyond his duties and that really bothered Jason. His philosophy was to always go above and beyond when kids are involved; they deserve nothing less. So he decided he'd keep an eye on things; if Kent didn't take the other kids' claims seriously he would at least look into them. There were ways he could do some digging from behind the scenes.

Later that night he sat in front of his laptop, looking for old articles on missing girls, runaways, and Jane Does. The information was disheartening; there were so many missing kids all over the state. He had to narrow it down to missing girls in the county of Grover. What happened next was very confusing: nothing.

Okay, maybe he needed to be more specific. He typed in reported runaways from Grover Homes group home for teens… Nothing again. But Jason knew that was not necessarily strange because runaways are not top priority, unless they're reported as missing, and many of the supposed runaways were close to adult age so they would quickly age out of the runaway file. He was going to have to try a new angle. Jason shut his computer down.

He could make an anonymous call to the missing persons department and ask if a Nikki Olson was reported missing… The thought was unsettling because, on the one hand, if she was never reported as missing then the director had blew him off, but what if he did report her and the police just didn't act? There were too many unknowns for Jason. He had to gather more information before he made a move. He had to speak to the ones at the heart of the issue.

The next couple of days were busy at the library. Jason not only had submissions coming in for the writing contest, but he also had to prep the large study room for the group that was coming in a couple of hours. He didn't mind the extra activity; he was actually looking forward to it.

The library had several large and medium-sized study rooms that the teachers and Grover Homes sometimes used to hold special classes; or a professor from the university would bring students in and hold a class or do research in them. He wasn't told all the specifics, but he knew the group was going to be working with some of the girls from the group home, and he was to make sure they had full access to the library. Kent Foster even spoke with him directly and asked if he could help in any way. Jason thanked him and told him he had everything under control. He didn't think the director was being insincere, and Jason decided that his encounter with him the other day was innocuous. Kent Foster was just another one of those arrogant rich guys with control issues.

Jason finished bringing extra chairs into the study room and decided to go find Tony. He and the precocious teen had a good bond, so he figured that would be the best person to start his inquiry with. He found him a few minutes later in one of his favorite aisles: science fiction/adventure, but he wasn't reading any book. Tony sat cross-legged with his folder beside him and a notebook in his lap, writing away.

"Hey Mr. J; I was going to come find you as soon as I finished," Tony said while he continued to write.

"Great minds think alike," Mr. J said as he sat down with his knees up in the aisle with him. "Let me go first, though." Jason inhaled and exhaled deeply, while rubbing his bald head. "We've come to know each other pretty well, I'd say, and I want you to know that I trust you. That's why I'm coming to you with this." Tony put his pencil in his notebook, closed it and set it to the side. Jason then told him about his conversation with Jamesha (leaving out her name) and he admitted that he got a strange feeling that something strange was going on over at the group home.

"I don't know…" Tony started, "but ever since I've been here there have been a lot of boys and girls running away; that's what most of us assumed anyway. I never put too much thought into it until now, but you know how girls talk—the consensus is most of those girls didn't run away. Some of the boys don't buy it either. Now they're saying Nikki ran—that little white girl—nah, I think there is something strange happening. Then you had what happened to us…" he told Jason what happened to Teresa the night they went out.

Jason didn't verbally respond to Teresa's incident, but his clenched jaw and narrowed eyes said enough. He did speak on their late-night tryst.

"Man, that's normal teenage behavior; you're supposed to be able to mingle with each other. Just keep it safe and teenage— none of you are in positions to take care of any kids. Okay, so what you and Jamesha told me is the same, and hearing the details, it doesn't sound like this was some kind of opportunistic, random attack; whoever this guy was, he was lurking. Is Ashley the girl you're closest to here?"

He didn't notice Tony blush when he said yeah; he was too focused on the beginnings of a plan.

"Here's what I need you to do: ask her which of the girls I should talk to with knowledge of who or what gang is heavily involved in trafficking women in the state."

"That would be Teresa," Tony cut in, "we've shared a little of our past when we were all hanging out and she mentioned some gang or clique that ran her town; you'll have to ask her the name."

Jason mulled over the information for a moment. "Do you think she'd be willing to talk to me about it? Will you ask her for me? This is just a hunch, but if nothing else, maybe she could lead me to others who know more."

"Yeah, no problem, I'll talk to Ashley today and see if she'll ask Teresa if she's cool with talking to you," Tony said. Confident that this was a good starting point, Mr. J changed topics.

"So why were you going to look for me?"

"I have my piece ready to submit, I wanted to give it to you personally and not just drop it in the submission box on your desk." Tony grabbed his folder and dug out the poem.

"A, don't think I'm gonna give you preferential treatment just because I like you," Mr. J said, "I gotta keep this fair."

"Hey, I'm not asking for any handouts. I let my work speak for itself; if someone does better they deserve to win," Tony said as he handed over his poem. Mr. J took the poem and smiled at him.

"That's what I'm talking about; character at its finest."

When his eyes fell on the page and he read the title he immediately snapped to attention; his posture became rigid and his hand trembled slightly. Tony saw his reaction and thought he was joking around, but as he studied him closer he realized Mr. J wasn't playing.

-The Dream Weaver- by Tony McNeil
Controlling reality begins with closing my eyes;
When REM state is reached
I breach remnants of paradise
Or torments like perdition
At this level of living
I'm so alive;
There's a peace within these scenes
Most call dreams—
I see them as guides
A paradigm behind a guise;
To be understood by the wise.
Designed to impart intuition,
Not superstition in the mind.
So many go against the vision;
Afflicted by symptoms so they miss signs.
Time? Never was.
I've sifted through outside influence,

That has created internal buzz:
The five senses, past experience
And all feelings including love.
Shutting down my connection to this world
Has led me to a world above.
I've reached a higher plane
Without the use of any drugs…
I met the Dream Weaver
And played cards with The Hands of Fate;
Learned that the deck isn't stacked
And anyone alive can crochet.
That's not to say,
One can't switch scenes
In the attempt to escape
The day to day monotony
That permeates the mundane.
Some days I've lived scenes
That would make some want to stay;
A memory so vivid
It becomes hard to separate.
I'd rather not distinguish,
But to linger
Would cause me to estivate.
Is it safe?
It's no more pernicious
Than a walk across the street
Although, blinking towards your wishes
Won't leave you fatigued,
But the trip is only useful
When you understand what you've seen.
Me… I've come to
Drenched in a cold sweat;
Tears came too
And left my pillow soaking wet.
Yet, some nights I go to a place
Where the joy is so true;

Rapt by the experience—
My soul is imbrued.
I hold on to what seems vacuous,
But enough to produce.
Unconscious consciousness
Has brought the Dream Weaver through.

"Are you alright, Mr. J?" Tony asked. Jason was so engrossed with reading the poem that he just grunted in response to Tony's question. When he finished he looked up at Tony with squinted eyes as if trying to see through him or like he was looking for something in him.

"Uh, Mr. J, are you alright, man?" Tony asked again, a little nervously, though. He hoped he wasn't having some kind of prison flashback.

"Where did you learn this?" Mr. J finally spoke.

"What do you mean, 'where did I learn this?' This is my poem. I came up with it myself; it's original!" Tony said with indignation. He was no plagiarist and he took offense at the insinuation.

Seeing Tony bristle at the question, Mr. J realized he worded it wrong. "No, no I meant where did you get the idea from? The Dream Weaver, who or what inspired that?"

"Oh, sorry," Tony said, feeling ashamed for snapping. But then he realized what Mr. J was asking and instinctively became guarded. He didn't get the feeling that he needed to hide the fact that he could dream weave from Mr. J; he hadn't done it in a long time anyway. But there was some internal defensiveness that kicked in when it came to the dream topic.

"Uh, it's just a piece I pulled out of my imagination. I dream a lot, you know, so I thought I'd come up with something different; something whimsical," Tony babbled.

Jason Madison was a pretty perceptive person, so he noticed once Tony understood the question, something in him changed; he was coming off too indifferent, almost evasive.

"This is definitely not a whimsical poem," Mr. J said, "This was something you put together with very much thought, or, on the other hand, it just flowed out of you because it is you: your thoughts, your experience. And that makes it even more profound, because there are layers of esotericism all through it."

Tony knew Mr. J was too sharp to try to fool, but he'd let him expose his hand first before giving in. It wasn't that he didn't trust Mr. J; this was just new territory.

"Let me level with you Tony. Do you know why I chose dreams as the topic?" Tony shook his head. "I've been fascinated with dreams for many years, in fact, it borders on an obsession. The only one I know more obsessed with the dream world than I am is Leon; it was Leon who opened my mind up to exploring some… let's say unconventional ideas about dreams and the power they possess. Your poem is the quintessence of those ideas. It's kind of eerie, like you've listened to our conversations and put them together in a coherent poem."

Tony began to let his guard down; the more he listened the more intrigued he became. He started to wonder if there could be others like him out there.

"See," Jason went on, "the first dreams I remember having were so vivid and intense that they made me think about them all the time. But my dreams never complete themselves, I've never had a dream play out fully, they always veer off. This might sound crazy but, I feel like if I could have a full, complete dream, it would somehow manifest itself in the real world… literally bring my dream to life." Jason sighed and rubbed his head. "You probably think I'm nuts huh?" he said with a dry chuckle.

"No, I don't," Tony said with a gravity that stopped Jason short. He looked at Mr. J squarely then said, "I don't think you're nuts. Finish telling me what you know and I'll… tell you what I can."

"Do you believe in the Bible Tony?"

Tony thought about it for a moment. "I don't know enough about it to believe in it or not," he said thoughtfully.

Jason shook his head and laughed a hearty laugh from the depths of his gut. When he saw the confused look on Tony's face he stopped and explained himself; saying that's the best answer he's ever gotten from that question, because most people just say yes or no. Tony didn't quite know how to take it so he just sat there and waited for him to continue.

"Well, in the Bible it says that God made Adam, the first man, out of the dust of the ground, but when he made Eve, the first woman, he caused Adam to fall into a deep sleep and then took one of his ribs out to make her."

"Why didn't he just make her out of the same dust?" Tony asked.

That's a good question," Jason said with a grin, "some Historians and Philosophers have said that this story was originally a mythical story that encoded spiritual teachings. And they say it was later tweaked by the male-dominated church to justify, and even promote, the inferior treatment of women. But, Mystics say the deep sleep Adam was in was REM sleep and he dreamed Eve into existence out of his own desire for companionship. Likewise, all of the stories in the Bible, where people had visions that came true, were actually people who were initiated into some kind of dream-world secret society. In fact, it's said that all the Arts and Sciences were learned by those who visited the dream world and had contact with divine beings there. But no one seemed to know where the idea of affecting reality with one's dreams came from. That is, until we were able to study ancient Egypt; it was clear they were the source.

To them the dream world was known as the Duat—the universal subconscious and unconscious. When they slept, they could communicate with the spirits and the Divine by accessing the Duat; this was known even by the everyday people of ancient Egypt. But there were those among the commoners who could tap into the Duat at will! Those who lived exceptionally virtuous lives and adhered to the teachings of the sages could raise the vibrations of their minds and sort of bend reality to their will. Of course there's a flipside. There were those who tuned into the Duat egoistically—with bad intentions—, whose worldly ambitions were so strong the energy turned inimical and granted the mind adverse or destructive abilities. Some believe you don't actually have to be asleep to dream or tap into the Duat—meditation was the most common means of entering Transcendental consciousness. No one knows for sure though." Jason rubbed his bald head and blew out a long breath. "You still think I'm not nuts?"

"Yes, you're sane. But you might think I'm nuts… I know a Dream Weaver." Tony prevaricated.

"And I suppose you're going to keep their identity a secretary huh?"

"I think that's the only respectful thing to do, but I'll mention you to them if you want,"Tony said.

"Yeah, do that for me Tony," Mr. J asked humbly.

So the old man was right, Jason pondered. Now that he had an outside source to corroborate it, albeit a very unlikely source, he felt relieved to know that his obsession was grounded in reality… somewhat. He felt like he should be excited, but he wasn't; he felt oddly serious, almost emotional.

"It's your turn now, Tony. Tell me everything you can."

"I don't know any of the mystical stuff you know; really you know way more than I do. All I know is… dream weaving is real and so is Neith," Tony said.

"What do you mean? How do you know?" Mr. J asked eagerly, eyes focused and searching.

"That's all I can tell you right now, Mr. J."

Jason knew this kid knew more but he obviously wasn't ready to share it; he would respect that and not push.

"Alright Tony, you've answered more of my questions than you know and I admire that you would honor your friend and keep their secret safe."

Tony felt bad having to deceive Mr. J; he really considered him a friend now. But he couldn't override the feeling that compelled him to guard his secret until he absolutely knew the person was… safe? Trustworthy? Mr. J was all of that to Tony.

"Well, I'm going to go get ready to met the counseling group," Mr. J said after he looked at his watch, "They should be here in about twenty minutes. This is one discussion I'd love to continue. Anytime you want to know more or share more you know how to find me."

"Yeah, we can definitely pick this back up and hopefully I'll have more to share—" Tony suddenly stopped and snapped his fingers, "The Syndicate, that's the name." Mr. J asked what he was talking about. "The gang Teresa told me about—it just came to me."

"Thanks. Make sure you talk to her for me; I won't approach her without the green light from you." Tony said he was going to the school and he'd be able to talk with her then. He got up with his book and folder under his arm and then left the aisle with Mr. J. He was going to talk to Ashley and have her give Teresa the heads up and then go back to his room and read the entire book on the Goddesses.

"So how's it gonna go down tomorrow? Tony asked when they arrived at the front desk. He held it in check, for the most part, but he was excited about the upcoming contest. Even if he didn't win 1st place, the exposure and the possibilities were enough for him.

"We're going to have all you guys and girls that entered the contest come to the big conference room, here in the library. The teachers will do the introduction speech and then I'll call the participants up one at a time and have them recite their work. After everyone who wants to share their work is done I'll announce the winners and award the prizes." Tony said that it sounded real professional as he headed for the exit. "One other thing: Grover Press offered to print the winners for a whole week," Jason added.

"What!" Tony exclaimed, "Man that's the type of exposure we need. I have to win at least third place," he declared as he reached the big oak double doors.

"I think you've got a really good chance," Mr. J said with a wink. "Don't sweat it, just be ready tomorrow."

"I'm always ready." Still looking at Mr. J, Tony reached for the handle of the door to his left, but before he could grab it, the heavy, polished wood rushed in on well-oiled hinges and collided with him, connecting with the left side of his head. He went down with a groan.

CHAPTER 9

As the five women approached the library, Kadence saw a beautiful black girl walking up the path from the group home, towards the library too. Had the girl been there when she first noticed the path as they pulled into the lot? She quickly shrugged the thought off, though. This might be one of the girls participating in the program.

The girl made it to the entrance before the rest of them but she didn't go in. She moved off to the side by one of the perfectly trimmed bushes that stood on either side of the doors. She appeared to be waiting for someone.

"You ladies must be the Y.T.P. group," the girl said pleasantly as Kadence approached.

"Yup, my name is Kadence." She extended her hand.

"I'm Ashley," she said as she shook Kadence's hand. Everyone else introduced themselves too.

"Did you sign up for the program, Ashley?" Roselynn asked.

"No, I figured I'd wait to see what the others thought about it first."

"That makes sense; I would've probably done the same thing," Kadence said with a smile.

Ashley smiled back. "You have really good hair," she said. "What do you do with it?"

"Oh, thanks," Kadence said and ran her hand down her hair demurely. "I just wash and condition it and use Shea butter." Ashley gave her a look of approval. Beautiful and doesn't know it, she guessed.

"I know Mr. J is waiting for you girls, so I better let you go. I'm sure we'll see each other again; I hear this program might become a permanent thing," Ashley said as she stood aside and let Kadence and the others go before her.

"I sure hope so," Kadence said. "We'll be in the library for the next few days, so you can stop and talk to any of us if you want." With a little more force than she knew was needed, Kadence pushed on the library door. The big door moved with ease. She felt the door connect with something on the other side and then heard that something collapse and groan. She looked back at the others and winced.

"Oh no, I think I just hit somebody." She went to the other door, gently pushed it open and peeked in. She saw a boy lying on his back, holding the side of his head. Concerned that she might've seriously hurt him, she hurried in and knelt down next to him.

"Are you okay? I thought that door was going to be super heavy, that's why I pushed so hard. I am so sorry!"

The rest of the group filed in past Kadence.

"Hey, you must be the Youth Tutor Group and... Ashley. I'm Jason," Mr. J said as he walked towards them. "Yeah, those doors are deceptively easy to move; I've been meaning to tighten the hinges. Guess I'll put that on the list for today too." He looked down at Tony with a half hidden smile.

"I'm Roselynn Mackey," they shook hands. "Looks like one of my girls took out your boy there. Sorry about that."

"Don't worry about it; Tony's got a tough head. He'll be fine."

As if he heard Jason, Tony rubbed the side of his head like he was trying to remove a stain from it. "I'm alright," he said, "it was just a little bump." Kadence stood up and helped Tony to his feet. When they were both standing Kadence took Tony's hand away from his face to inspect the damage she caused.

"Here, let me see how bad it looks." Before she could look at it their eyes met. Time seemed to slow down; the other voices faded away and everyone and everything else disappeared. There was just Kadence and Tony; two childhood friends who were forced apart by tragic events neither one of them could control, now standing face to face after five years of not knowing the fate of the other.

As soon as their eyes locked they knew it was real—they found each other. But the suddenness of it was so overwhelming neither of them could find their voice right away.

"Oh… my… God… Tony…," Kadence breathed the words out in a heavy whisper.

"Kade'… what—' ' Tony began, but before he could get the rest out she wrapped her arms around his neck and stole the words from his mouth. They held each other tight, filling the void that had been in their young lives for too long; their embrace forging a promise to never lose each other again. The sudden poignancy of the moment was quickly noticed by everyone around them. Kadence had Tony in a tight hug with her eyes closed and tears streaming down her face. The other Y.T.P. girls stared, open-mouthed, at Kadence's sudden display of affection; they had never seen this from her before. Mr. J just looked confused.

"Did she hit 'em that hard?" He asked no one in particular.

"I'm not sure but… Kadence is known for her passion, that's what makes her so good with the tutor program," Roselynn said with admiration. Ashley, on the other hand, was far from confused. She stood to the side and watched the whole scene unfold with her arms crossed over her chest and undisguised jealousy on her face. This Kadence is, no doubt, the best friend Tony told her about. What's the chance she would be a part of the Y.T.P., and be so beautiful? Ashley was certain she would have no more competition once she scared off Brianna and a few others she thought had their eyes on him. She'd play it cool for now, though. After one last glance at Tony and Kadence she uncrossed her arms and headed towards one of the computer stations.

Jason was the only one to notice Ashley's internal struggle of whether or not to make a scene of her own or not. Thankfully she chose not to—he was not equipped to handle that scenario. He was struggling to grasp what was happening with Tony and this other girl.

"Um, Kadence, is everything alright here?" Roselynn asked gingerly as she approached them. Kadence and Tony let go of each other and returned to the present. Kadence wiped the tears from her cheeks and gathered herself. Her response was still raw with emotion.

"Yes, everything is fine, Mrs. Mackey. This is Tony McNeil, my best friend I told you about. I didn't know... I had no idea he would be here!"

Roselynn put a hand over her mouth in astonishment. She remembered very well the heartbreaking story Kadence told her about her best friend and how he was the main reason she wanted to be a part of the Y.T.P. She couldn't have known he was here —the way she told the story, she seemed not to know if he was still alive. This was truly amazing. "Wow, this is such a blessing. I'm Roselynn, nice to meet you Tony; I've heard a lot about you," she said with a warm smile.

"Hi," Tony said a little awkwardly from the extra attention everyone seemed to be paying him now. Jason cleared his throat from where he was standing a few steps away. Now that he had the gist of what was going on, he figured he could help out a little—Tony looked like he could use it.

"Tony is like my helper around here; he knows this place as well as I do. If it's okay with you, Roselynn, I could show you and the other three young ladies around, and Tony could show Kadence?" Mr. J finished smoothly.

"Yes, of course, that would be fine; Kadence is very responsible."

"Good, so is Tony. Shall we begin then, ladies?" With that Mr. J smoothly led Roselynn and the other three ladies—who were ogling him—in the opposite direction of the reunited friends, to begin their tour.

"I don't believe this! How did you find me?" Tony asked.

"I really don't know. For a while I didn't even know you were still alive. I mean, I've been asking about you ever since you stopped coming to school. You know, I don't think I found you—it's more like we were brought together. By who or what I'm not sure. But like my mom says: there are no accidents." Kadence reached across the table where she and Tony sat and squeezed his hand as if to assure herself he was real.

"Yeah, things went all the way downhill after Lisa and Tommy's funeral. You know, sometimes I wish I would've died too."

"I'm so sorry about your family, but don't say that Tony," she said.

"It's true. And why did she keep me alive anyway, to be alone? To learn something? What's the lesson in that?! I don't get it," Tony said bitterly.

"She?" Kadence asked with raised eyebrows.

"It's complicated. You're the only person I had left when my mom died and… and when them people came for me I knew I lost you too."

Kadence sat in silence for a few moments before speaking. "No, you didn't lose me. And even though I thought you were gone… for some reason, I still felt you with me. It sounds like some movie junk, I know, but that's the only way I can explain it."

He knew exactly what she felt because he felt it too.

"I know why you're still here: you weren't meant to die." She paused and looked him squarely in the eyes before she continued.

"I know what you did for my dad, Tony. I know it was you. I know because you left a part of your gift with me."

She told him about her dreams and the way she could see into other people's past through them; all of their true thoughts and emotions. And she told him exactly when it started. When she finished, Tony sat silently for what seemed like minutes and then he told her everything.

"I knew it, I knew it was you! Why didn't you tell me before?"

"Because I knew I had to—I have to—be careful with who I tell. There's something, a strong resistance or overprotective feeling that hits me anytime dream weaving is brought up. It's weird, though, because I didn't get that feeling with you just now. I actually felt like I needed to tell you." An airy warm feeling of relief settled over him, making him breathe out the last word as he finished. The weight of the secret he carried easing from his shoulders and with that feeling came clarity as Kadence continued.

"I think it's because you transferred a piece of yourself to me when we were kids. But, it wouldn't have mattered if you told me or not—I knew it was you!" She finished matter of factly and they both laughed.

"So how long are you here for and exactly why are you here?" Tony asked her. She told him all about the Youth Tutor Program, her plans, and what they'd be doing over the next few days. They asked each other a lot of questions, laughed, and shed a few tears.

Kadence eventually looked at her watch and remembered her obligation. Tony told her he could give her a quick tour of the library on her way to the large study room they would be having their groups in.

"Make sure you stop by on my breaks. I think Roselynn's giving us a half hour after the first group, and she said we can be in the library all we want when it's open," Kadence said as they stopped together, right before they arrived at her destination.

Tony let her know that he practically lived in the library so they would definitely see each other. They hugged and Kadence kissed Tony on the cheek. "See you later Dream Weaver."

CHAPTER 10

"You know we hear things in here before you guys do—most of the time."

"Yeah, I know Old Man. Did you get the letter?" Jason asked.

"That's why I'm calling, Jason. What, you don't think I have anything better to do with my time?" Leon said with mock indignation.

"Did you take your Milk of Magnesia? I know you get kinda cranky when you're not regular," Jason said with just as much mock concern and a huge grin he knew the old man could see through the phone.

"I don't need that junk; I push it out all on my own. Thank you." Jason laughed. Glad to hear the old man hadn't lost a step. "What you asked me about in the letter is a yeah," Leon said as the levity dissipated. "Listen son, I don't want you gettin' involved in none of that mess, though. Leave it alone!" he cautioned sternly.

"Are they really that serious?" Jason asked skeptically.

"Do you remember your third year here?" Leon answered.

"Yeah, I remember every year—oh, that was them?" he finished somewhat impressed as he remembered the specifics.

That summer a correctional officer was making his rounds, walking down a tier by himself, when a prisoner who was leaning against the guard rail shoved him in an open cell with another prisoner, and then slammed the cell door shut. It happened so fast and unexpectedly that the C.O. never had a chance. When the other officers finally got up to the fourth tier, minutes later, the prisoner who pushed the C.O. in the cell started fighting with them. When they subdued him and made it to the cell, the officer inside was on the floor; his face nothing more than a puddle of blood, grey matter, and skull fragments. One of the other guards threw up right in front of the cell. The guy who fought with them laughed out loud from where he was handcuffed to the ground. Another guard walked over and kicked him in the face and the guy just spit out a few teeth and laughed harder. The prisoner who just brutally murdered a guard was calmly sitting on his bunk watching his TV, bloody fingers clicking away at the remote.

The story was that the guard was dirty and owed money to some very connected people. People Jason was now inquiring about.

"Yep, that was them, so whatever it is let it go," Leon warned again.

"It's too late for that—I'm already in it," Jason said resolutely. The old man sighed. Hearing the intrepidity in Jason's tone, he knew the youngster was set to do whatever it was he planned on doing. "They're messin' with kids out here—young girls Leon!"

As they both paused, an understanding passed between them. Leon knew Jason had a soft spot for kids because of his past and he would never be able to stand by and let them be mistreated if he could do something about it. He admired him for that. But that didn't stop him from worrying. The truth is, Leon had come to love Jason like he was his own son. Behind that façade of grumpiness, Leon was comforted to have Jason in his life; he gave him purpose.

"You stay on your toes out there; these people have a long reach and they're heartless," Leon said ominously. "They're not like those other petty street gangs, fighting over colors or street corners, and they're not just black or white; they're everybody in between too."

"I will Leon. These kids need some help and right now it seems like I'm the only one listening to them. I gotta do something." He let out a sigh and rubbed his head. "If I can help in some way, without landing on these guys' radar, that's what I'm going to do but…"

"Yeah, I know—"

"YOU HAVE ONE MINUTE REMAINING." The automated voice chimed in, signifying the ending of their call.

"Well, I'm gonna go get my laundry. You make sure you keep me posted son, and tell that sharp youngster I said keep reading."

"I will. Hey, Leon?"

"Yeah, son?"

"I love you old man."

"Love you too, kid."

Leon Bradford is an old school convict; he's been in prison so long no one that was on the transfer bus with him when he was first brought in is still alive. So he's no stranger to prison etiquette; he knows how to "bid" as the convicts call doing time. He was twenty-five when he came in; he did the young and wild thing for a few years: smuggling, drinking hooch, etc. He quickly made a name for himself, which was I'm-not-the-one. The white supremacy groups tried several times to recruit him. A simple no thanks was like speaking a foreign language to them so they got to meet I'm-not-the-one more than anyone else. He did a couple years in the hole on a few occasions and the different gangs and racial groups eventually got the picture—Leon Bradford wasn't interested.

Forty-two years later, Leon or Old School, as all senior convicts are called, was known as the most likable, good-natured guy in the system. He was sought out for sound legal advice and other general information. The guards knew and respected him and in the usually segregated environment that permeated all prisons, he knocked that barrier over. He wasn't the kind of person who claimed not to see color, though. In fact, it was just the opposite with Leon: he saw it more vividly. He noticed the differences and similarities between races and he didn't see anything in one race that made it better or worse than another. He wasn't ignorant of the racial tension; he just chose not to let it dictate who he was and how he did things.

Leon no longer had to stay on guard for potential threats of payback or some guilty-by-association drama; he could do his time peacefully. Having Jason in his life went a long way in adding to that peace and it gave him a sense of accomplishment that he'd never know otherwise. Now Jason's altruism was threatening that peace.

Feeling guilty for his selfish thoughts as he did his laundry, Leon reflected on the phone call. He knew Jason was intelligent and was doing the right thing, but he also knew that getting into the Syndicate's business has never had a good outcome.

Caught up in his thoughts, he didn't notice the approach of a skinny white guy, with slicked back dirty blond hair and bloodshot eyes from snorting a combination of psychotropic medications. As Leon pulled a shirt out of the dryer he didn't register the sudden movements until he felt the sharp pain rise in his side. He thought the guy just bumped into him until his breathing became labored and he found himself on the floor, finding it harder and harder to keep his eyes open as someone started yelling for the guards.

CHAPTER 11

Second place—not bad Tony," Javontay said from his top bunk.

"Man, he shoulda got first place! The thing was rigged— that's why I didn't get in it," Marcus dramatically proclaimed as if it was he who got robbed of a first place victory.

"Nah, Tay's right; that's not bad at all. Out of thirty-four submissions I made second place, and there was some good competition too. Did you see the twins' performance?"

The twin girls, Charvay and Charday, had angelic voices. They sung a beautiful ballad about the hundreds of young girls in Nigeria abducted by the terrorist group Boko Haram, and how their dreams don't seem to be as important to the rest of the world because no one came to their aid. What was even more impressive was how they convinced the panel of teachers to let them participate in the contest because technically it was a writing contest, but, as they argued, they did write the lyrics and they even included a short but factual introduction on how lots of girls and women in some parts of Africa are denied education and therefore the chance to live their dreams. They got first place.

"Yeah, they did snap, though," Marcus said with sincerity and all hints of indignation gone. No one spoke for a while as they lay in their beds, thinking of what was to come. None of them wanted to be the first to bring it up, but like the natural leader he is, Tay broke the silence first to address what they had to do.

"Are y'all ready for tomorrow night?" Tony said yeah and Marcus said he was more than ready. "Make sure we stick to the plan. We can't let him get too close to Mesha—we have to get him first, so he can't use her as a hostage or something. And remember: bum rush him at the same time! Once we have him down Mesha is gonna start screaming," Tay instructed. Tony and Marcus let him know they understood.

"If he's got a gun, though, everybody scream—I'm not trying to get shot."

Joseph Greycloud doesn't dream very often, but when he does he's left with the feeling that he has experienced or witnessed something profound; something he was meant to understand. Metaphorically or literally, he didn't know.

His dreams were so vivid and moving that he didn't realize they were dreams until he woke up, and even then he felt as though they were memories of something that really happened. This night's dream was no different:

"One boy cradled another's head as he sat beside him, where he lay on the ground. Though the one being held didn't cry out, the tears leaking from the corners of his eyes and the contorted grimace on his face was evidence of the excruciating pain he was in. Joseph could tell that the pain was not just physical—it was that heart-wrenching emotional kind too.

'I'm not gonna leave you.' There was kindness as he said it, but the words were devoid of any pretense; he knew he was dying.

'I know you wouldn't leave me... you've always had my back. But... I'm leaving you. I'm sorry.' The boy labored to get the words out through his pain. His breathing slowed and his eyes drooped…"

Joseph woke up sweating profusely, with tears in his eyes.

"You stay right there, Marcus and keep your eyes on the right side of the building. I'll be behind that tree, watching Jamesha. And Tony, you go to the far left side in case this dude comes from that way." Tay finished, pointing to a cluster of trees almost hugging the left corner of the girls cottage. Tony asked what if the guy comes from behind them.

"That would probably be good 'cause we could jump 'em before he ever got close to Jamesha," Marcus answered.

"As long as he doesn't see us first," Tay shot back dryly.

"But chances are he's coming from where the roads and highway are—there's too many trees to get through. Still, keep your peripheral vision and senses on point," Tony said. "And," he added, "Marcus, keep that shoestring ready so we can tie him up quick once we got him on the ground." Marcus assured him that he had it.

"Y'all ready?" Tay asked and looked at each of them. They returned his intense look and nodded.

Jamesha knew the other girls were asleep; they had talked for a while—long enough to where each one slowly faded into silence. It was time. She quietly reached for the outfit she had prepared. As she dressed she kept glancing at the other two girls—one more than the other—making sure not to make too much noise, but enough to let anyone listening know she was up. When she finished tying her shoes she went to the window and looked out.

Being honest with herself, yes she was nervous and a little scared, but she had to do this. She wouldn't let what almost happened to Teresa happen to another girl if she could do something about it. She took a deep breath and focused on slowing her pounding heart down, and then she lifted the window and climbed out.

Tony and Javontay saw her first, since they had the job of watching the side of the building her room was on and her, respectively. She climbed out the window with ease and started walking towards her destination. Jamesha walked unhurriedly but with purpose; not wanting to look like she was expecting something. Tay, though, could tell she was nervous by the way she kept touching her hair.

As she walked, going towards the main cottage, she passed the other girls' windows. She didn't notice that one of them was open. She got no more than a few steps beyond it before someone stealthily emerged from it and immediately backed against the building to conceal themselves in the shadows.

Tay, Marcus, and Tony all looked each other's way, unsettled and caught off guard by what they saw. Tay held his hand up, signaling to them to hold their positions. They didn't know who that was; it could be a girl for all they knew. Jamesha, apparently secure in knowing the boys were close by, didn't look back. Meantime, the unknown figure kept to the shadows and followed her.

All of a sudden Jamesha stopped and looked as if she wanted to turn around and start running but was stuck. Someone was running full speed towards her, showing no signs of stopping. At the last second she found her mobility… it was too late though; the person running at her ran past, bumped into her and plowed full speed into someone who she never knew was mere steps behind her. They went down in a tangled mess.

"Marcus!" Tony yelled as he and Tay sprinted as fast as they could towards him, Jamesha, and whoever Marcus was now tussling with on the ground. Right before they made it, Jamesha let out a piercing scream that cut through the silent night. The other figure disengaged from Marcus and took off in the opposite direction they were coming from.

"He's hurt, Tay! He got hit with something; oh, my God, oh my God!" Jamesha said frantically from where she sat a foot away. Javontay knelt down beside her and held her as she trembled and cried, holding onto Marcus's arm. Tony knelt next to his friend as he struggled to get up. When he touched his chest to keep him still, he felt the warm sticky wetness of blood.

"He stabbed me, Tony… it hurts… bad. But, I'll be alright; just give me a minute to catch my breath," Marcus said as he looked his best friend in the eyes. Tony sat on the ground next to Marcus and gently picked his head up and cradled it.

"Tay, go get someone to call 911—hurry," Tony said calmly without looking up. Javontay let go of Jamesha and bolted to the front of the cottage, yelling for the staff the whole way. Jamesha inched closer to Marcus and Tony. "I'm not gonna leave you," Tony said as he felt his friend weakening.

"I know you wouldn't leave me," Marcus gritted through his pain, "You've always… had my back. But, I'm leaving you, just like everyone else in our lives left us. Sorry." His breathing became harsh and in the dim moonlight, Tony could see the blood seeping out the side of his mouth. Then his eyes closed.

No matter how adamant he was about swearing to never dream weave again, he was more determined to never lose a loved one again. Period. Under no circumstances was he willing to accept the loss of someone he cared for. The ache in his chest rivaled that of the wound in his friend's; the pain Marcus must have felt when that knife plunged into his chest coursed through him, causing him to shake. If he wasn't meant to use his gift for moments like this, then he didn't want it. What was the use? Neith could have it back.

Without a warning, Tony slouched over Marcus like an off-balanced sack of potatoes and didn't move. Waking consciousness faded in an instant and Tony entered the realm of dreams. His emotions and thoughts were already so focused on Marcus and his predicament that he was instantaneously there, in his sub mind; the only part active after he lost consciousness.

Tony saw the thread that linked Marcus to life being frayed. He reached into Marcus's dreams and they welcomed him in; surrounding him like a bunch of translucent crystal wind chimes, dangling all around him and flashing thousands of scenes. He zeroed in on the one exuding a tremendous amount of pain.

As he entered the scene, he felt the pain—he became the wound—and he knew what he had to do. He examined himself and saw that the knife had cut into his chest cavity, nicking the bone and leaving a piece floating around. Tony extended his mind outwards and reeled the fragment back to himself and wove it back into his skeletal structure. He saw the puncture in the lungs and stitched it closed, then he focused on the muscle and finally the skin, healing the sensitive vascular inner mesodermal layer and then the epidermis. When he felt complete and void of pain, he withdrew. The crystal wind chime-like scenes returned and Tony now saw Marcus in his own dream world. Marcus was at a barbecue, holding a plate and waiting in line. Suddenly he looked up towards the sky and Tony knew what he was looking for. He retreated back into his own mind and darkness enveloped him.

"Tony, what's wrong!" Jamesha screamed, after he suddenly rolled off of Marcus unceremoniously, arms locked straight out and his fists tightly clenched.

Just then, Tay came running back with Michelle, the female staff working the overnight shift. Jamesha was still yelling, trying desperately to understand what was happening.

"I don't know what's wrong with him," she said, "he was just talking, and then he rolled over like that."

"He's having a seizure," Tay said as he looked at his friend. When the three of them moved into their room together Tony told them that he had a history of seizures and described in detail what to look for and what to do. He only said something because the staff told them the coveted single bed was his. Tay and Michelle quickly went to him. Tay held his head while Michelle turned him on his side.

"My God, where is all this blood coming from?" Michelle asked worriedly.

"It's from Marcus," Jamesha answered.

As if on cue Marcus sat upright and looked around at the commotion surrounding him. He first noticed his best friend on the ground next to him, jerking with his face contorted and being held in place by Tay and a woman he didn't immediately recognize. Then he noticed Jamesha a few feet to the left of him looking disheveled, distraught, and confused.

Tony's episode subsided and Michelle gently roused him; he came to disoriented, irritable, and sore. Marcus was the only one looking at him though; everyone else was looking at Marcus. He looked down at his bloody shirt, put his hand where a mortal wound used to be and gingerly felt around. A cut in his shirt is all that was there; no soreness or even a mark on the skin. He didn't understand what happened, and as he looked around, it was clear no one else did either.

"Okay, help me get Tony up and let's go inside and wait for the ambulance. Then we can figure out what exactly is going on," Michelle said, breaking the silence.

As they all began walking around to the front of the girls cottage Jamesha stopped long enough to pick up something that crunched under her foot. She gasped when she got close enough to the light to see what it was. Everyone stopped and looked at her.

"These are Nikki's," Jamesha almost whispered as she held up the pair of mangled Chanel frames.

Inside the girls cottage, most of the girls were up, talking amongst themselves in their own little groups in the day room. They gasped when they saw the blood on Marcus and Tony. Ashley ran over to them as soon as she saw them.

"What happened to Tony? What's going on?" she asked in a higher than usual tone. "Why is he bleeding? Tony what's wrong?!" She made her way, somewhat forcefully, to where they had helped Tony to a couch, and knelt down beside him as he lay on it.

"No one's bleeding, Ash. I just had a seizure; I'm alright though, really," Tony assured her.

"Where's Teresa?" Marcus asked Ashley after he scanned the room for her and couldn't see her anywhere in the midst of any of the other girls.

"I don't know. She wasn't in our room when I got up to see what was going on out here." Marcus looked at Tay and he looked just as unsettled. "Where are your rooms at?" Marcus asked Ashley and Jamesha.

"Hold on, you can't go in the girls' rooms," Michelle said flatly.

"Man, somebody has to go check on her. We just saw a grown ass man try to snatch Jamesha!" Marcus yelled. Many of the other girls heard him and they looked terrified, covering their mouths in shock and huddling closer together.

"Jamesha, please—" Michelle started then stopped as Tony began convulsing again. "He's having another one. Damn, where's the ambulance," Michelle said, starting to feel very overwhelmed.

Tay helped her with Tony again while Ashley looked on with worry and Marcus and Jamesha left to search for Teresa. Seconds after they left the ambulance could be seen and heard pulling up. A few of the older girls went outside and guided the paramedics into the house and straight to Tony who was still in the grips of a seizure. They asked a few questions as they loaded him on a gurney, then brought him out to the ambulance and drove off.

"She's gone," Jamesha said when she returned to the day room with Marcus.

"Who's gone?" Michelle asked.

"He took her," Marcus said with tears coming down his face.

"Who?" Michelle persisted.

"Teresa," Ashley, Jamesha, and Tay said at the same time.

Marcus hung his head down and his friends went to him and put their arms on and around him.

Chapter 12

Yeah, he probably did see me—the moon was kinda bright. But it doesn't matter anyway; I stabbed him in the chest... hard. There's no way he survived that."

"Well... our people said he's still alive. In fact, our people are saying some strange things indeed: the boy you stabbed had a lot of blood on him, but he didn't have a single scratch on his body. So tell me, Bronson, what you stabbed him with?!" Semion spoke with a force that seemed to shake the room. Standing only inches away from the man that outweighed him by at least seventy-five pounds, Semion had his hands clasped behind his back.

"Semi, I'm telling you, I stabbed him. I had no intentions of doing it at first, but he was a lot stronger than I anticipated and I heard more of them coming. I had to get away and eliminate the only person who might've seen my face," Bronson carefully explained.

"So it seems Cassandra set you up twice," House said, standing nearby.

"No, the first time was my fault—I grabbed Cassandra instead of the other girl. But this last time... they were waiting for me,"

Bronson answered, clearly annoyed that some kids got the drop on him and that House was rubbing it in.

"Yes, it does appear that our Cassandra has defected. Seeing as she is nowhere to be found; I would say definitely. But I believe you Bronson; I believe you did stab him," Semi said and put a hand on the man's shoulder reassuringly, instantly easing the tension in his upper body. "But someone else is involved, someone… powerful, and we just can't risk them finding out who you are because that of course would lead them to me. Others are already meddling." Semi removed his hand and turned away. As he did, House, who went unnoticed by Bronson, slipped a garrote around his neck and yanked back.

Bronson struggled futilely against the three hundred forty pounds that was House. He went down to his knees, clawing at his throat and then his arms went limp. House held him a bit longer, and then he dropped him on his face.

"Here is what I know: whoever saved that boy's life lives there with him and they are interfering with my research—that I cannot allow. But…" Semi paused and flashed a crooked smile that didn't reach his eyes, "whoever it is, has just maybe led me directly to what I've been in search of my entire life. That boy was not saved by conventional methods. There is no more room for errors; we are too close now. Use our contacts to find out everything about that boy. And when you're done here I have a special task for you." With those final words he left House to clean up both Bronson, and the messes he left before and after his demise.

He was so close, he could feel it. Bronson wasn't sloppy when it came to carrying out a job; Semion Djaneve knew that—that's why he hired him. But the reports he received from his inside sources were clear: there was a lot of blood yet no one had any wounds; an ambulance was called for a person with stab wounds, but when they got there all they saw was a boy having back to back seizures.

As far as Semi was concerned, the boys are non-factors, unimportant. It's the girls—the dark skinned girls—that hold the real power in their melanin. He returned to his office and unbuttoned his shirt, forcing himself to be patient; he had to calm himself so he could be prepared for the dangerous journey he was about to embark on once again.

He went to a small refrigerated incubator that kept its contents at body temperature and removed a vial. He took his shirt off, then sat in his chair and stared at the dark leathery patch of skin on his upper left bicep. In his quest to find something powerful enough to transport him to the collective consciousness and give him the power to challenge reality through it, Semion had been injecting and topically applying all sorts of chemicals and drugs during his meditation sessions. Most recently, it has been highly concentrated neuromelanin from young black females, the very stuff in the vial he now held. This, by far, has yielded the greatest results. But, it is very volatile and requires the utmost control and focus or the person using it will not survive.

Semi centered his thoughts and went through his regular pre-meditation ritual: slowing his breathing down to a sleeplike rhythm. When he felt ready, he took a fresh razorblade from his desk and made a deep gash in the form of a cross right in the center of the patch. The skin in that area had become so tough and scarred that it took much longer than normal for any blood to swell to the surface. When it did, it was very dark and it rose like dough, staying in place and not running like normal blood would.

Semi watched it carefully, uncapped the vial with his teeth and poured the entire vial where the opening of his wound crossed. He spit the cap on his desk, dropped the empty vial and quickly put his right hand over the wound and clamped down tightly. His eyes closed, and then shot back open, showing only the whites. His jaw clenched tight and he lost all sense of his surroundings.

But he was conscious; only his consciousness shifted to a parallel realm.

He saw an image of himself standing in the midst of nothingness; impenetrable darkness surrounded him. As he continued to look at the image, the image began to change. And he felt the change. His eyes bulged, his skin bubbled up in horrific blisters, oozing blood and yellow puss, and his scalp started to peel back—the pain was unbearable! Semi tapped into his will and forced himself to pull away from the gruesome image of himself. When he did he saw what looked like millions of stars floating in space. He centered his thoughts on one person and as he did, one of the stars brightened and then appeared right in front of him.

He stepped through the star and was engulfed by images so strong, so compelling that it took all of his willpower not to fall into them, and believe he belonged to them and therefore be consumed by them. He focused on his breathing to find his mental equilibrium and stave off the onslaught of forceful images, feelings, and thoughts. Confident of his control, he allowed himself to look around.

Semion saw Cassandra; her thoughts, plans, emotions, and hopes; images of who she loved and hated, all surrounded him. He filtered through it quickly, knowing he couldn't linger for too long because if he did he would be absorbed by her life force energy and completely obscured from existence. He withdrew and found himself back in the midst of the impermeable darkness, littered with stars. He began going through the process of returning to body consciousness: retreating from the image of himself slowly until it blurred and the many stars became one bright light that eventually dimmed and winked out. He only backpedaled once before one of the many stars brightened like a supernova, making it very difficult, even painful, to look at. With every fiber of consciousness and mental energy he possessed, he concentrated on that supernal star. Like before, the star appeared in front of him, but unlike the other one, when he tried to enter, it would not let him in. And though it was bright, he felt like he was looking through stained glass. He strained to see whatever he could. Semi saw what he knew was a memory, a childhood memory, before he was forced to retreat. He didn't have to backpedal—the energy surrounding this star pushed him all the way out of the dream realm.

He returned to the material plane exhausted, as usual. His hands trembled violently as he reached for the Valium on his desk. He wouldn't be able to move for at least a few hours. The journey was taxing every time he went to the otherworld, but this trip took more out of him than usual. It also yielded more answers, though.

CHAPTER 13

"Hi, may I speak to Jason Madison please?"

"Yeah, this is him," Jason said through a sleep laced voice.

"This is Jennifer Berberick at the Department of Corrections and—"

"Jenny?" Jason said with surprise and a little more excitement than he wanted to expose.

"Yes, Jennifer Berberick," she replied with curt professionalism.

"Hey, it's good to hear from you, but what's going on?" he asked skeptically as he picked up on the personal detachment in her tone.

"Well, I'm here at the prison—" she emphasized, Jason thought, "and I'm Leon Bradford's case manager. I'm sorry to have to inform you that Leon was attacked… he's on life support. You are the only person listed as his emergency contact person— the only person listed in his files that is still alive actually."

"Hold on, this has to be some kind of mix up. Someone attacked old man Leon? What?! He doesn't have any problems with anybody; what happened?" Jason was stunned.

"I'm sorry Jason, but because of the ongoing investigation I can't give you any details. I can only tell you that he was attacked with something sharp—most likely a shank—and the prognosis isn't good. I'm sorry Jason."

Jason heard the sincere compassion in her voice. He sighed in disbelief as the situation really started to sink in. "So can I see him or what am I supposed to do?"

"Right now, the facility is still locked down —you know how that goes—but an exception should be allowed if we get the approval from the warden. I'll work on that as soon as we hang up."

"Thank you. Damn, this is really messed up; Leon hasn't done anything violent since before I was alive!"

"I know this is a really hard time for you, but please be patient and I will call you with any new information I get." He thanked her and she told him to take care. Jason hung the phone up, numb with a mixture of anger and pain, and the biggest sense of helplessness he'd ever felt. But as the gears started turning in his head, he felt a sickness settle in the pit of his stomach. He had a good idea why this happened to the old man.

At work, later that day, Jason decided he would act on the thought he'd been pondering all morning, since he got the call from Jenny. He picked up the phone at the desk and dialed.

"Grover Homes, this is Carter. How may I help you?"

"Hi, this is Jason Madison at the library. Can you connect me to the Dover dorm staff please?"

"No problem, hang on a sec."

"Dover dorm, Joe Brinley speaking."

"Joe, this is Mr. J. I was wondering if you could let Tony McNeil know that I just got the book he needs for his test this morning, so he can pick it up before class." Joe said he'd send him over when he's ready. Jason thanked him and they hung up.

Jason distractedly started checking in returned books while waiting for the boy to arrive. The thought of taking the day off never crossed his mind when he got that dreadful call this morning. He knew the mechanical motions of checking books into the computer and returning them to their correct aisles would help him work through his mixture of depressing feelings better than sitting at home would. And he somehow felt something could be done from here.

One of the books he was scanning had a piece of notebook paper sticking out from it. Thinking it was probably one of the kids', he looked it over, checking for the name of its owner. When he saw the name at the bottom he became alert and really read it.

Tony came in about twenty minutes later, but Jason was so absorbed in his thoughts that he didn't see him standing at the front desk.

"Uh, I don't have a test today, Mr. J. What was Brinley talking about?"

Jason slowly looked up and blinked a few times. When he spoke, his exhaustion and weariness were evident.

"Yeah, Tony, I know you don't have a test. I needed to see you and I figured that was the quickest way without raising suspicion."

"What's going on?" Tony asked with concern. "Did you find out something about the girls?" He definitely noticed a different look on Mr. J's face—he looked… sad.

Mr. J rubbed his face with both of his hands, exhaled and looked at Tony with an intensity that held him in place. "Sort of, but right now I need your help Tony. Leon is in trouble; he was hurt really bad." He briefly paused and then blurted out his request. "Tony, I need you to ask your friend for help; Leon didn't deserve this and I know it's my fault—I should've never gotten him involved. I didn't want to bother you because I know you've had a really rough past few days… but right now, I don't know what else to do; I'm desperate."

"You know," Tony said, "I've never had two seizures that close together like that, and Teresa… man, it's pretty scary around here."

"I know. I can see it on the girls' faces," Mr. J said sadly. There's something else that just came up too, but I'll give you time to reach out to you friend. And I really think Jamesha should be here when I show you because she did come to me first."

"Mr. J—"

"Hold on, Tony, let me finish first. I don't know what your friend, the dream weaver, can do to help Leon—if anything—I'm just asking that he or she do whatever they can. Anything at all," Jason finished with undisguised desperation in his voice. Tony promised that he'd do whatever he could and Mr. J thanked him.

"Can I take that picture of Leon with me—for my friend?" Mr. J reached in his back pocket and pulled his wallet out and found the old prison photo. He handed it over to the boy without a question. "Do you mind if I bring Marcus and Javontay... so we can all see what you have to show me?"

"Yes, I think you should all be there."

Tony made his way back to his cottage; he timed it so that Marcus and Tay would already be at school when he got there. When he got to his room, he shut the door and put a chair under the door handle. Then he went to his dresser and pulled out one of the small pills the doctor recently prescribed him. He'd been taking an adult dosage of Depakote, an antiepileptic drug, every morning since his last episode. At first, he wasn't sure about continuing to take it because he didn't know what it would do to him or his ability, so he cheeked a few and hid them. After reading everything he could find on it in the library, he felt comfortable enough to start taking them again. Plus the doctor stressed how important it was that he take them because having back to back seizures could cause permanent brain damage and in some cases death. He popped the thousand milligram tablet in his mouth and swallowed it without water.

He walked over to his bed and lay on his back, and then he pulled the picture of Leon out and stared at it. Tony traced the wrinkles on the old man's face with his eyes and studied his slightly bent frame that had obviously been strong a long time ago, but now looked vulnerable and weighed down. Tony thought about the conversations he's had over the phone with Leon; the inflections and the energy he gave off. He closed his eyes and was instantly there, in Leon's dreams.

He was surrounded by tall shelves stacked with books higher than he could see over. Tony looked all around, and then stopped as he noticed an open book suspended in midair in front of him. The book seemed to be at its end, on the very last page. This was no regular book, though. There were no words, just images of Leon's thoughts, emotions, desires, memories, and dreams— what is, was, and could be. It dawned on him then, that everyone must display their dream world in a different way; a way unique to them.

This last page in Leon's book was showing Leon as he currently was: hooked up to an oxygen machine, with an IV in his hand. Tony reached out and touched the page. As soon as he made contact he entered the scene—he became the scene.

As he lay on the hospital bed, he felt the blood flow to his brain being restricted. He concentrated on the blockage and saw the tiny blood vessels that were collapsed; he opened them up, allowing the oxygen back in and the neurons to start firing again. While the shank didn't hit any vital organs, it did cause sepsis which severely weakened his immune system. Tony focused and gathered the infection together, and then expelled it from his body, right through his pores, leaving not a trace of it. He felt himself getting stronger; energy surged through him like an electrical charge.

He withdrew his focus and found himself surrounded by the tall bookshelves again. As he peered at the books on the shelves, he noticed that the bindings, where the title of the book would normally be, were transparent, allowing him to see into each one. He found Leon's dream and as he watched him carry out his everyday routine he understood that it was the simple things that brought him the most joy: eating a good meal, participating in the programs that let him mentor younger guys and most of all, getting letters and visits from Mr. J and seeing his passion for working with kids. A great sense of fulfillment radiated from him and that moment, Tony felt warmth of his own course through his being.

He released Leon's dream and brought himself back to his own consciousness. His eyes flew open. He was sweating heavily, but he wasn't having a seizure. He stood up on shaky legs, went to the door and moved the chair. He started to open it and go to school but he quickly decided against it. He could miss a day.

CHAPTER 14

He sat on a dingy brown couch that had so many stains, it appeared to be two-toned. Upon closer inspection, one would see the old oily grease marks for what they were. They didn't bother him though, in fact, he almost looked just like the couch: light brown with slightly darker blotches under his eyes and spread over his body from lack of sleep and old scars. The matted black curls on his head were just as greasy, and the caked up crust in the corner of his eyes was reminiscent of the old food crumbs one would find wedged between the cushions. His once wiry frame, with squared shoulders, was now slouched and soft like the sagging cushions on the couch. And his mood matched it all.

This young guy, in his early thirties, aged considerably in just a few years, from inactivity and a poor diet of Seagram's Gin aka Bumpy Face. He currently held a half full bottle by its neck in one grimy hand as he absentmindedly watched an infomercial about a magic wrinkle-smoothing cream. It didn't matter that it was in Spanish and he couldn't understand a word of it; in reality that probably made all the difference. Words he could understand caused him to think and with thinking came too many memories—painful ones that reminded him of who he once was and all he lost. He brought the Bumpy Face to his lips and took a long swig. A few years ago his life changed horribly and he lost everything. He should be gone too, but by some mistake or a cruel joke by God, he was still here. He didn't possess the strength or weakness it took to take his own life, in any of the conventional ways, so he slow-rolled it with the Bumpy Face gin. He took another swig.

He didn't work, didn't have to now because he collected a disability check. Some type of stress disorder caused by the accident. He dismissed it, though, and just went along with the monthly psychiatric visits so he could get his check every month. The way he allowed the gin to saturate his liver, he knew those visits wouldn't last too much longer. He was knocking on death's door; death just seemed to be ignoring him. He brought the gin to his lips again, but stopped before he took a drink. Was he that wasted or was he actually hearing knocking as he drank his life away? Oh well, he thought, maybe death is ready to answer. He took a pull from the bottle and coughed as it caught in his throat. Much to his irritation, and disappointment, the knocking—that just turned into banging—was on his apartment door.

"Nobody's home!" he yelled as he wiped the liquor from his mouth with the end of his dirty muscle shirt. The knob turned, and since he never locked his door, it swung open with ease. He turned his head towards the door with a flurry of biting words on the tip of his tongue, ready to thoroughly cuss out his nosy old neighbor who always seemed to find an excuse to come check on him. The words never made it past his lips and the huge man that just entered his tiny apartment was not his neighbor.

"You know your door was unlocked, T? I know you're not in the projects anymore, but this is still the ghetto," the huge man said admonishingly. T stared up at the big man for a long moment as if his eyes were deceiving him.

"House?" The word came out so garbled, it sounded like he said couch. The big man looked at the squalid couch and brushed nonexistent dirt from his clean black hoodie.

"Nah, I'll stand," he said.

"House," T said again and this time it came out clear.

"Who else would it be, the black Kool Aid man? Damn, T, what the hell have you done to yourself? When's the last time you took a shower? You smell and look like shit!"

T grunted, picked up the gin and took another sip. Yep, this was House, his old hustling partner. He didn't know how he found him, but he wasn't too surprised. Although House is 6'5", three hundred-plus pounds, he's far from lazy and he always finds whatever or whoever he's looking for.

"Man, you really let yourself go—"

"What do you want House?"

"I don't want nothin'."

"Then get out and leave me the hell al—"

"But…" House cut back in. "The man has a job for you; something to help get you back on your feet." T swigged from his bottle and glared at the big man.

"Tell the man I 'preciate the offer, but I'm straight. I get a check every month and this," he held up the bottle, "is all I need to help me get on my feet."

"A check?" House said with disgusted consternation, "It ain't stretchin' far enough. That couch looks like it's literally growing on you. Look man, I know you've been through some serious shit, but you gotta—"

"You don't know a gotdamn thing! And I ain't gotta do nothing but sit here and get drunk," T said vehemently and then started to take another drink. But with remarkable quickness that belied his name, House reached across the rickety table and snatched the bottle from T's feeble grasp. He took it to the kitchen where T could hear the liquid being poured down the drain and House loudly muttering imprecations at the filth he encountered.

T smiled stupidly, like only a drunk could, as he thought about the two unopened bottles in the cabinet above the sink. The smile faded as he heard house rummaging through the cabinets; he tried to get up but couldn't seem to find his footing so he gave up. House would leave and he'd go buy some more.

"What are you trying to prove?" House asked as he conspicuously dropped the empty bottles into the plastic trash bin, and then walked back to the living room to resume his position in front of the couch. "That you can drink yourself into a coma? No, I get it: you're trying to kill yourself."

The veracity of his statement hit home and caused T to focus his bloodshot eyes on the big black man.

"You wanna drown in your sorrow and then give up huh? Well here, let me help you out; we can save us both some time." He reached a meaty hand under his hoodie and came out holding a .44 Bulldog revolver, loaded with six Hydrashock bullets.

T didn't waver; he continued to stare at House defiantly, hoping the giant was going to take him out of his misery. No such luck. House placed the gun on the table and T's stare faltered.

"There you go, homie; it's all yours. One shot will do it. This way you won't have to drink any more of that nasty ass gin. Go ahead."

T slowly reached for the .44, trying to hide his trepidation but failing miserably. His hand was shaking so bad he'd make a Parkinson's disease patient feel sorry for him. When his hand was directly above the gun it hovered there tremulously.

He couldn't do it. He didn't even have what it took to pick the gun up, let alone use it. House called his bluff, but more than that, he forced him to face the fact that maybe he couldn't do it because deep down he really didn't want to die. And that thought made him feel guilty and ashamed. He withdrew his hand, slowly squeezed it into a fist and gently set it in his lap and then he closed his eyes and let go of the breath he'd unconsciously held in.

"You know why you can't do it? It's not your time. I can't front, you've been through some heavy shit and you lost a lot. But don't disrespect their memory by giving up the life you've been allowed to keep. Life ain't over for you. Stop feeling guilty for something you had no control over and take charge of what you have left."

House picked up the gun and put it back in his waistband as he watched his words penetrate the dense fog of depression and despondency that hung over the pathetic man in front of him. He knew he still had a long way to go, but he was in now. He had a job to do and failure was not an option—not when Semi wanted something done.

"Man, I haven't seen you in years and then out of nowhere you come here with a job offer. I'm not in the hustling shape I used to be in, as you can see; so what is this job?"

"Well, it took some time finding you; you don't go out much. I'm not the one offering the job though, so he'll have all the details. And you're damn right, you ain't in shape to do a damn thing, so first things first. I got some coffee in the car, then you gotta get cleaned up 'cause you're not sitting in my car smelling like that. We'll start there." House headed for the door, then stopped and turned back, rubbing his chin thoughtfully.

"What?" T asked with raised eyebrows.

"I was going to say welcome back but... we have a while to go before you're back." He shook his head ruefully and left the apartment, thinking of the pain this man has endured all because of one bad move, and the second hell he would soon face when he found out the truth.

CHAPTER 15

Many times in my life I've felt like I've had too much on my plate, like I was in over my head. Some people may think being able to dream weave should make life easier, but actually things are more complicated. It takes so much out of me; I feel a part of myself leave every time I do it. But I feel like I have to use this gift to keep the people around me from dying, even if it is killing me. I couldn't save my family, but maybe I can create a new one by giving myself to those who are here now. But at times like these, when the people I love are going through so much pain, pain that my dream weaving can't heal, I feel so overwhelmed and useless.

"Are you sure Teresa wrote this?" I asked.

"This is her handwriting and her signature; I know it is for sure," Marcus said, clearly confused. And Jamesha concurred. Tay said damn, expressing with one word what everybody was feeling.

"Maybe someone forced her to write it," Kadence suggested. Over the past few days the girls got to spend a lot of time with the Y.T.P. group. Most of them seemed really comfortable with

Kadence in particular. So when Jamesha, Marcus, Tay, and I met Mr. J in the library and she saw us sitting down as their group was leaving for the day, no one objected to letting her in on the discussion. She asked Roselynn if she could stay a little longer. Mr. J offered to give her a ride back to the hotel and Roselynn okayed it after Kadence reminded her that this was their last day.

"Here, read it for yourself. In my opinion, this seems too well written and thought out to be forced," Mr. J said as he handed the paper over to Kadence. She took it and read it out loud.

"Late submission: Living My Dream

These days I'm finding it more and more difficult to keep my eyes open. Some would say I'm trying to run away from something, and if I was honest, I couldn't disagree. It's not that I'm feigning fatigue; my exhaustion is real, even though I do sleep. See, every moment my eyes are open I'm forced to live a nightmare; I have to see the facade I have erected just to survive, and it hurts. It hurts constantly trying to escape the pain of my past, but then reliving it anew by lying to those I love; spreading more pain.

So every time I get the chance, I close my eyes, because when I do, the nightmares that chase me during the day aren't there. Dreams rule the darkness, limitless possibilities roam the unconscious mind and I become what I am in my heart: a young woman who has endured so much adversity, but has risen above and not been corrupted by the evil she has felt and seen. A young woman who knows she is beautiful, not because a man told her so, but because she sees it herself every time she looks in the mirror. A young woman who can resist the temptation to give in and fight for herself and those around her...

But, as my eyes open my dreams flee and the cold reality of my waking nightmare takes hold once again: I'm a young woman that has been drowned by my struggles and turned rotten by the wickedness I grew up around. I am ugly because of the ugly things I have done; all the while convincing myself I had to do them if I wanted to survive. I am weak and I caved in a long time ago; unable to fight for myself without throwing others in the way of harm so I could make my escape. I've never done a courageous thing in my life, but today… I'm going to chase my dreams with my eyes open and save someone other than myself. My dreams will rule the day."

"This is heartbreaking," Kadence said and wiped a tear from her cheek, "but it's really good. Yeah, she wrote this because she wanted to—she needed to. It sounds like she held this in for a long time."

"It doesn't make sense, though!" Marcus said. "The guy tried to take her, remember? And she was really scared."

"Unless she was acting," Tay said impulsively.

"What?!" Marcus said, taken aback.

"I've seen it before," Jamesha said.

"Yeah, me too; girls are really good at that," Kadence agreed.

We all looked around at each other, not really knowing what to think about it all.

"Think about this, though," Mr. J said, breaking the silence, "you guys said the guy was bigger than me. Why didn't he just man-handle you all and take Teresa? None of you girls are big enough to put up a real fight against a maniac who's determined to take you. You said it was dark, right? Well, maybe he didn't mean to grab Teresa? It sounds like he gave up pretty easy to me; so maybe he realized he grabbed the wrong girl?"

"Damn!" Tay and Marcus said at the same time.

"Where's Ashley?" Kadence asked, and an uncomfortable silence passed between us.

Before this meeting we were all unsure what role Ashley played in this mess. Jamesha made it clear that she didn't trust her, and after I talked to her and heard what everyone else thought, I had to admit that she did seem suspicious. But after this, I really didn't know what to believe. I don't want to believe she's involved, though.

"Yeah, I was just thinking the same thing," Mr. J said and looked right at me.

"Well," I began, "after everything went down the first time, we all talked and… we all thought Ashley's response was a little odd; she didn't seem fazed by what happened."

"Actually, that's not that unusual," Kadence said, "many girls become blase when they've endured a lot of trauma at an early age. I've worked with some girls who have talked about horrific things that have happened to them like it was normal."

"I think this changes everything, though," Mr. J said. "Clearly Teresa is involved in some way, or she was and no longer wants to be. What's more concerning to me right now though, is we don't know how deep this goes or who else is involved. So what I need for all of you to do is keep this between us. We don't know what we're dealing with or who we can trust. Okay?" We all agreed.

"Another thing: I don't want you guys going anywhere alone." He looked at his watch. " I know I've kept you here a little late, but the library closes in about twenty minutes and it's already dark outside, so why don't you hang out a little longer and I'll walk you all to your cottages." We liked that idea too.

As we started walking off Mr. J called me back and I told Kadence I'd catch up with her in a minute. She caught up with Jamesha and left Mr. J and I to talk.

"Thank you, Tony." His gratitude was so heartfelt that I almost said you're welcome, but I remembered to feign ignorance just in time.

"For what? What did I do?" I asked in my most mystified voice.

"Whatever your friend did worked, Tony—it really worked. Leon is okay, better than okay! The doctors can't even explain it; they want to study him. They say they've never seen a person recover as fast or as thoroughly as he did, in his condition. Your friend is the real deal. Thank him for me please."

"I will. I wasn't telling a story when I told you I knew a dream weaver."

"Do you know what this means, Tony? Your friend could change the world—"

"But at what cost to him?" I said, and immediately regretted it. The question stopped Mr. J's effusion of utopian thoughts and he seemed a little ashamed when he spoke.

"I… didn't even think to consider what your friend goes through or how much of a burden this might be on him. I mean, if the wrong people, or especially the government found out there was someone that could do what he did there's no doubt they'd try to control him or experiment on him at least."

I hadn't even thought that deeply into it, but he was right, and it just reinforced my protectiveness and reluctance when talking about dream weaving.

"It's not as easy as it might sound; he's really drained afterwards," I said. I was almost certain he knew it was me when we first talked about goddesses and dreams. Now, I had the feeling he knew for sure and was pretending to be ignorant like I was.

"Tell your friend I really appreciate what he did, and if he ever needs anything, I'll do whatever to make it happen. And don't worry; his secret is safe with me." I said I'd tell him. "Go catch up with your friends and you guys meet me at the front doors in about ten minutes. I'm going to shut down the computers and lights."

I found Kadence sitting with Jamesha, Marcus, and Tay. When she saw me coming she excused herself and met me halfway.

"So, how are you holding up?" she asked.

"Okay, I guess. I haven't had another seizure since I started taking the meds. What about you? It's crazy around here huh?"

"Yeah, there's a lot going on—too much. I know I'm going to sound kind of selfish saying this right now, but I really want to spend more time with you. I'm leaving early in the morning; it went by way too fast!"

"I was thinking the same thing. Do you think your dad will let you come back to visit?"

"You know, I called him and told him I literally bumped into you. He sounded real happy, for him anyway. He asked about you… I told him you got tall. I think he will let me come back; he's not as grumpy as he used to be."

The lights started going dim and flicking off one by one. We all began migrating towards the front doors. Kadence reached her hand towards mine in the dimly lit library, and without the slightest hesitation, I grabbed it and held it as we walked. When we made it outside, Mr. J told us to wait for him before we headed back on the path that led to Grover Homes.

"I'm telling you now: if somebody tries it with all of us out here, then we know we're dealing with a crazy person!" Jamesha nervously joked.

"They'd have to be pretty stupid indeed," Mr. J said. I think hearing him say it the way he did made us walk with a bit more confidence.

We dropped Jamesha off at her cottage first. We all hugged her and made sure she was inside before we headed off to the boys cottage. When we got there, Tay and Marcus said their goodbyes to Kadence and a see you later to Mr. J, and then they went inside.

"Who's working tonight, Tony?" Mr. J asked. I told him I think it's Mr. Brinley. "You two hold on; I'll be right back." Kadence and I just looked at each other and finished talking. A few minutes later Mr. J came out of the cottage with a barely perceptible grin on his face. I wondered if he and Mr. Brinley were friends outside of this place.

"Alright, let's go; I promised Roselynn I'd get Kadence back a.s.a.p., Tony."

"You have my number and my address now, so call and write—" As she spoke I closed the distance between us and put my arms around her.

These past few days I realized that Kadence was more than my best friend; she is the only person I have left from my past, the one person linking me to a time and place I long for but can never get back. But, with her, I have a big piece of that place returned.

She returned my embrace, and then with her arms still holding me, she pulled back. When I did the same she looked into my eyes.

"I love you Tony. Don't ever forget, you'll always have me."

"I love you too, Kade." She softly kissed me on the lips and hugged me again.

Mr. J cleared his throat loudly. "I'm trying to make a good impression on Miss Mackey, but y'all are going to get me chewed out if we're late. Let's go." Kadence and I laughed and reluctantly let go of each other. I watched as Kadence and Mr. J started walking away. Mr. J stopped all of a sudden and turned around.

"Are you coming or what?" He asked with a grin.

"What?" I was caught off guard.

"What do you think I went in there and talked to Joe about?" I hurried and caught up with them, and we joked and laughed all the way back to the library parking lot, where Mr. J's truck was parked.

CHAPTER 16

Help me put her in the middle of the road, T."

"Man, I just watched you pick her up with one hand; you don't need my help," T said as he got out of the truck to help House.

"I see that the accident didn't damage your ability to complain," House remarked, unruffled by T's griping.

He trusted House… as much as a hired hand could be trusted. But, trust or lack thereof was not why Semi decided to accompany his most loyal man on this mission. No, this mission was special and required his personal touch, and Semi very much believed in the adage, "if you want something done right, do it yourself." There was no room for any mistakes here; he would ensure there were none.

Chapter 17

Being in the backseat of Mr. J's SUV with Kadence as we traveled down the dirt road, leaving the group home, felt like a road trip. We didn't get to leave the Grover Homes grounds very often, unless you were one of the lucky ones who got home visit passes. Or, like me, had to go to the hospital. Right now, being with Kadence and Mr. J, I felt normal; like this is where I belonged. It was bittersweet though, because I was dropping my best friend off, not knowing when I would see her again. Yeah, she said she'd come back and visit, and I believed her, but things don't always turn out how we plan them. And I knew, as soon as I got back to Grover Homes, the reality of my situation would hit me like a ton of bricks and the empty space in my life would return. But for now, I'm living in the moment and enjoying the ride.

The truck suddenly skidded to a stop, throwing Kadence and I against our seatbelts and kicking gravel and dust up. We jerked forward, almost hitting our faces on the front seats.

"What the heck Mr. J—" I said from the back seat.

"There's… something in the road. Stay here; I'll be right back." He jumped out of the truck and ran over to whatever he'd almost run over. Seconds later he yelled for me to come and give him a hand. I told Kadence to wait in the truck and I'd be right back. When I got to where Mr. J was kneeling I stopped short and sucked in my breath.

"Teresa? Is she… dead?" I asked him.

"No, she's unconscious and beat up pretty bad. Grab her legs and help me get her to the truck."

"Wait a second," I said. Mr. J didn't protest, he just watched me curiously as I closed my eyes…

Nothing happened. I couldn't shut my waking consciousness down and enter the dream world! I knew then that the pills I was taking did affect my ability. They must've built up in my system the longer I took them. The price for dream weaving had to be paid; the seizures were the price and I had to go through them if I used my gift. I opened my eyes.

"Come on, we have to get her to the hospital," I said as I picked up Teresa's legs. When we made it back to the truck, the back door was open.

Mr. J asked Kadence to grab Teresa's head as he guided her upper body into the backseat. "Kadence?" Mr. J said as he looked around the inside of the truck and didn't see her.

"Where did Kadence go?" Mr. J asked me after we got Teresa in the truck.

"She's supposed to be in here; I told her to wait for us." This all felt really wrong. I yelled her name out.

"Kadence is fine Tony, she probably went—" Mr. J and I both stopped and looked in the same direction. Standing in the middle of the road, at the very edge of the beam of the truck's headlights, stood the biggest man I've ever seen in my life. And he had my best friend. Kadence wasn't that short, but standing in front of this guy she seemed childlike.

"See, she's just fine," the huge man said. Mr. J and I started to walk towards them. "But…" the man said, pulling a gun from his hoodie and putting it to the side of Kadence's head, "that can and will change if you keep walking my way." The way he said it wasn't menacing; it was all business and that's what made it even more convincing.

"What do you want with her?" Mr. J asked calmly.

"Me? I don't want anything with her."

"Then why don't you just let her go; she hasn't done anything to—" Mr. J stopped as a pair of headlights came into view behind the man holding Kadence at gunpoint.

"But, there's someone else who does," the man said. The car stopped just behind the man, then a person got out of the passenger's side and then the driver got out too.

"Why did you do that to the other girl? It's obvious you used her to get us to stop, but you didn't have to hurt her like that. What's really going on here?" Mr. J said.

"Well, it seems Cassandra developed a conscience at the wrong time for her and the opportune time for me," one of the new people responded in what sounded like an African or Jamaican accent.

"Her name is Teresa and she's just a girl; you didn't have to do that to her!" I was so mad I was shaking as I yelled at him. Whenever this medication got out of my system they would be in trouble.

"Ah, you must be Tony. Well, Tony, her real name is Cassandra. She used to work for me—I promise she is not the girl you think she is." This new information caught me off guard. How could Teresa—Cassandra—work for someone like this? And how did he know my name?

"So what do you want?" Mr. J asked. "We can resolve this without anyone else getting hurt."

"Of course we can; I am a very reasonable man—"

"Let Kadence go; she hasn't done anything to you!" I demanded.

"You are right, she hasn't. No need to worry; I have no intentions of taking her anywhere; although her dark skin is very rich and would definitely yield a potent batch. But, I have actually come for something else; someone much more special."

I don't know what this guy was talking about, but he sounded sick, like he would cook her and eat her or something. I had to get Kadence away from these people. "Well, let her go; we won't interfere. You can go get whoever you're looking for," I said, hoping by tomorrow I would be able to dream weave.

The Jamaican man chuckled. "Thank you, but I have already got who I'm looking for. It is you. I have come for you Tony," he said. The dread that washed over me almost knocked me over, but I overrode it. I would do anything to get Kadence away from them; even if it means I have to take her place.

"I can't let you take him." Mr. J said and put a hand on my shoulder protectively.

"I do not believe that is your choice to make, Jason," the man said lightly.

"He's right, Mr. J, this is my choice and I choose Kadence." Mr. J took his hand off my shoulder and hugged me. He whispered in my ear that he would be coming after me.

"Get Teresa to the hospital. Kadence will know how to find me; she knows she can trust you. I'll be okay Mr. J," I whispered back, and then let go and started walking towards the other car. I stopped halfway there and yelled for them to let her go.

"Sure," the Jamaican man said, and the big man holding Kadence released her. She sprinted to me and hugged me as hard as she could. She was crying and trembling in my arms.

"Please don't go, Tony, please!"

"I have to Kadence; I can't let them take you. You know how to find me… use your gift. Mr. J will help; you can trust him—"

"Tony?!" A new voice yelled. The other man who had been standing there walked forward, shielding his eyes from the headlights. "Tony Dasan McNeil?"

I haven't heard my middle name since I was a little boy. I turned towards the other man, who like the other, I couldn't fully see because of the glare of the headlights.

"What the hell is this? What do you want with my boy, Semi?!" After he got the last word out, the man who had just released

Kadence, grabbed him and though he struggled fiercely, the big man didn't give an inch. "Let me go House!"

"Sorry T, it's just business," House said calmly.

"Speaking of business," Semi said, "Tony is in possession of something I've been in search of for a very long time, and I will have it."

"What could he possibly have that you want?" T asked.

"That is not your business—"

"That's my damn son, so it is very much my business!"

"Dad? How? I thought… you died." I was so stunned my knees felt wobbly as I took a step forward. My dad stopped struggling and hung his head down.

"No… I survived. The night your mom signed the forms to take me off life support I started recovering; I woke up a couple days later. But… she was already gone."

"Why didn't you come get me."

"I couldn't. I wanted to but… I just wasn't in any shape to have you with—"

"We really must be going now, but you two can discuss this later. You'll have plenty of time," Semion said.

"No, you're not taking him!" My dad yelled. House knocked him in the side of the head with the barrel of his gun and my dad fell to his knees.

"Let me let you in on a little secret then: the only reason you still have a son is because of me! I spared him!" Semi yelled back.

"What?"

"Think about it Thomas. Do you really think I would just let someone steal from me and get away with it? Come on, you gave yourself away when you started buying cars, selling weight and paying your son's medical bills with cash. No, that wasn't a car accident. But, I showed mercy—I told my guys to leave you in the coma and leave your woman and son alive." Semi paused and flashed a cruel smile. It is quite fortunate, for both of us, that I stayed my hand."

My dad was moaning and making these pitiful whimpering noises; sounding like a wounded animal. All the fight was gone from him. I was furious though. At my dad, this Semi guy, and the big man who worked for him.

"Kadence, go with Mr. J," I instructed her and then watched her until she was in his arms, then I walked towards the Jamaican. "I'll go with you; just let them go. I won't fight you," I said.

"I know you won't," he said soothingly and before I knew what was happening, his hand shot up to my neck and he stuck me with something.

"You'll be fine; just a little something to help you get some sleep… without dreaming."

CHAPTER 18

"Please, please wake up Tony!" The voice pleaded with sadness and longing. This sad, young girl sounded far away but very familiar. "We really miss you. I can't even pay attention in school; every time Miss Mary reads, it reminds me of you, and I start crying." The voice paused and sighed before going on.

"I try to hold it in; it's really hard though. Granny said when you wake up she's gonna spend a lot of time with you. She cried a lot yesterday and said she felt like she neglected you. I don't know... I just want you to wake up so you can come back home."

The voice stopped and seemed to walk away, and then speak in a hushed tone to someone else. "I have to go now, Tony, but I'm coming back after school tomorrow. I promise," the voice said. I felt a small hand take hold of mine and gently squeeze. Seconds later I felt a soft kiss on my cheek, and the voice, much closer now, spoke again.

"Sweet dreams. I love you." At that moment I knew who that voice belonged to. With all my might I tried to squeeze the little hand that was still holding mine. I must have been somewhat successful, because she started screaming.

"Mom, Momma; Tony is holding my hand! Hurry up and look at this, Mom!"

"What is it Lisa?"

"Look mom, he's holding my hand—he's waking up."

ABOUT THE AUTHOR

Antonio Williams is the founder of T.O.N.E U.P Inc, an organization based in the Minneapolis and St. Paul areas, dedicated to serving Black and Brown people returning to their communities after incarceration. He is a founding member of The People's Canvass, a worker owned Cooperative that does year-round community engagement, canvassing and organizing. He wrote for The Spokesman Recorder and won an award for his short fiction through PEN America in 2018. He is currently weaving his next dream…